ALSO BY SHIRLEY ANN GRAU

The Black Prince and Other Stories
1955

The Hard Blue Sky
1958

The House on Coliseum Street
1961

The Keepers of the House
1964

The Condor Passes
1971

The Wind Shifting West
1973

Evidence of Love
1977

*These are Borzoi Books
published in New York
by Alfred A. Knopf*

NINE WOMEN

SHIRLEY

ANN

GRAU

A L F R E D — A — K N O P F

NINE

S H O R T

S T O R I E S

WOMEN

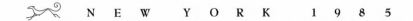 N E W   Y O R K   1 9 8 5

This is a Borzoi Book published by Alfred A. Knopf, Inc.

Copyright © 1985 by Shirley Ann Grau

All rights reserved under International and Pan-American Copyright Conventions.

Published in the United States by Alfred A. Knopf, Inc., New York,

and simultaneously in Canada by Random House of Canada Limited, Toronto.

Distributed by Random House, Inc., New York.

Grateful acknowledgment is made to Little, Brown and Company for permission

to reprint an excerpt from _The Complete Poems of Emily Dickinson._

Edited by Thomas H. Johnson. Copyright 1929 by Martha Dickinson Bianchi;

Copyright © renewed 1957 by Mary L. Hampson.

Library of Congress Cataloging-in-Publication Data

Grau, Shirley Ann.   Nine women.

1. Women—Fiction.   I. Title.

PS3557.R283N5   1986   813'.54   85-40340

ISBN 0-394-54845-0

Manufactured in the United States of America

First Trade Edition

A signed first edition of this book has been privately printed

by The Franklin Library.

CONTENTS

NINE WOMEN

THE
BEGINNING

In the beginning there was just my mother and me.

"You are," my mother would say, "the queen of the world, the jewel of the lotus, the pearl without price, my secret treasure."

She whispered words like that, singsonging them in her soft high voice that had a little tiny crackle in it like a scratched record, to comfort me when I was a baby. Her light high whisper threaded through all my days, linking them tightly together, from the day of my birth, from that first moment when I slid from her body to lie in the softness of her bed, the same bed she slept in now. The one we took with us from place to place. And there were many different places. We were wanderers, my mother and I. I even had a wicker basket for my toys; I would pack and carry them myself.

It mattered little to me where we lived. I did not go outside. I did not go for walks, nor play on park swings. On the one day my mother was home, on Sunday, we worked together, all the while she sang her murmured song to me. Secret treasure. Lotus flower. And in her murmuring way she told me all she knew about my father, a Hindu from Calcutta, a salesman of Worthington pumps. Of all the many men my mother had known, he was the only one she had loved. She told me about his thin face and his large eyes black as oil, and his skin that was only slightly lighter than her own.

"You have his eyes and his skin," she said as, after my bath, she rubbed me with oil. (It was baby oil, its vanilla scent soon lost in her heavier perfume.) "And you have his hair," she said, combing in more oil.

And there is, to be sure, a certain look of India about me. Even now, in the grown woman.

"You are a little queen," my mother would say, turning me around and around. "You are exquisite, a princess of all the world. You must have a lovely new dress."

And so I would. She made all my clothes, made and designed. Summer dresses of handkerchief linen and soft smooth voile, winter dresses of dark rich velvets, and monk's-cloth coats so heavily smocked across the shoulders they were almost waterproof.

Of course we couldn't afford to buy fabrics like that, not in those days. My mother worked as a stock girl for Lambert Brothers Department Store. She had worked there for years, even before I was born. Ever since she'd come out of the country. (That was the way she put it, as if it were the bottom of a well or a deep hole.) And Lambert Brothers provided our material, quite a lot of it over the years. It all began on a city bus when my mother met a clerk from the Perfection Cloth Shoppe. They began talking, casually at first and then with purpose. My mother exchanged a bottle of perfume or a box of dusting powder or some Lancôme lipsticks from Lambert Brothers for small lengths of expensive material from the Perfection Cloth Shoppe.

My mother never told me how she smuggled the cosmetics out of the store. I suppose she'd been there so long and so faithfully that they half-trusted her. She did tell me how she and her friend robbed the Perfection Cloth Shoppe—a simple plan that worked for years.

My mother's friend collected the fabrics over a period of weeks, hiding them among the hundreds of stacked bolts. When she saw her chance, she bundled the pieces tightly and dropped them in a box of trash, making a small red check on the outside. My mother had only to pass along the service drive at the back of the building, look for the mark, remove the package. That evening we spread out the material on our kitchen table (the only table we had) and admired it together. Only once did something go wrong. Once the trash was collected an hour earlier than usual and my beautiful dress went to the city incinerator. My mother and I managed to laugh about that.

During those early years, during the long dull hours checking stock in dusty rooms, my mother began planning a business of her own, as dressmaker. My stolen clothes were the beginning. I was her model, the body on which her work came to life, the living sketchbook. Too small to see above the knees of adults, but perfectly quiet and perfectly composed, I displayed her clothes. My mother did not need to teach me how to walk or to act. Remember your father is an Indian prince and you are his only daughter, she would say to me. And so we made our rounds, peddling our wares, much like my father and his Worthington pumps. If he had traveled farther, half a world, our merchandise was far more beautiful. My mother and I went to talent shows and beauty contests, to church services and choir rehearsals. Wherever ladies gathered and the admission was free, there we were. My mother sold her clothes, as it were, from off my back.

"We are selling very well in the Afro-American community," my mother would say. "Soon I will open a small showroom. The walls will be painted white and the only thing on them will be pictures of you. On every wall, the entire way around."

And eventually she did just that. I remember it very clearly, the white room, quite bare and businesslike and lined with pictures of me. They were color photographs, very expensive for a woman just starting in business, but they showed the details of the clothes beautifully. My face, I remember, was rather blurred, but the light always seemed to catch the smooth line of my long dark hair. When I modeled for the customers (seated in creaking folding chairs and reeking with conflicting perfumes), my hair was always swept forward over one shoulder. My mother ironed it carefully in the dressing room at the very last moment. I remember the glare of the naked light bulbs around the mirror and the smell of singeing as my mother pressed my hair on her ironing board.

I don't remember saying a single word at any time. I have since noticed that people usually speak to a child, but no one spoke to me. Perhaps they did not think I was quite real.

Twice a month, in the evenings, my mother did her books. For years these were my favorite times. I sat, in my nightgown (always ankle length, always with a drawn-lace yoke), in the corner of the sofa, its red velvet worn and prickling on the sides of my arms, and watched my mother with her checkbooks and her account books and her order books. I watched her pencil picking away at the pages, flicking, stabbing, moving. She was a very good bookkeeper. In different circumstances I suppose she would have gone to college and earned a CPA to put behind her name. But she didn't. She just remained somebody who was very quick with numbers. And there was another strange thing about her, though I didn't notice it until many years later. She was so good with figures, she spoke so very well in soft tones as soothing as a cough lozenge—but she could hardly read at all. She wasn't illiterate, but she read street signs and phone books, business forms and contracts all the same way: carefully, taking a very long time, sounding out the words. As a child, I thought that muttering was the way everyone read. (The nuns at school soon corrected me.) Eventually I just fell asleep on the old sofa with that comforting whispering lullaby in my ears.

When my mother picked me up to carry me to bed, which was next to hers, she would always be smiling. "The figures dance so beautifully for me, my little love. The Afro-American community is contributing devotedly to the treasure of the mahal. The daughters saw her and blessed her, also the queens and the concubines." (Someone had once read the Bible to my mother; bits and pieces kept appearing in her talk.)

In the morning when I woke, she was gone. At first, when I was very small, when I first remember things, like wet diapers and throwing up in my bed, there was someone who stayed with me, an old old woman who sat in a rocker all day long and listened to the radio. Her name was Miss Beauty. I don't remember her ever feeding me, but I suppose she must have. She died one day, in her rocking chair. I thought she was asleep so I went on playing with my doll. My cat— we kept one to kill the mice that played all over the old house—jumped on Miss Beauty's lap, then jumped down again quickly, coming to sit next to me in the window. "You heard her snore," I whispered to the cat, very severely. "Don't wake her, she won't like that at all." At the usual time I heard my mother's key in the lock and the funny little nine-note tune she whistled every evening just inside the door. (It was from *Lucia di Lammermoor,* I discovered years later in a college music appreciation class, and I rose in my seat with the impact of memory.) I put my finger to my lips and pointed silently to Miss Beauty. My mother hesitated, eyes flicking between us, nose wrinkling like an animal. Without moving, she bent forward toward Miss Beauty. Then quickly, so quickly, with a clatter of feet across the linoleum floor, she snatched me up and ran outside.

After Miss Beauty's death, there was no one. I stayed by myself. We moved to a nicer neighborhood, a street with trees and double cottages behind small front gardens. (The landlord had paved over our garden with pale green cement.) I never felt afraid. If I got lonely, I could sit in the big front window and watch the neighborhood children play in the street. I never joined them.

During these years I do not remember my mother having any friends. I remember only one visitor. He was short and wore a plaid coat and a wide-brimmed hat, and the ring on his left hand flashed colored lights. He was waiting for my mother when she came home after work. They talked briefly, standing at the curb next to his big white car, then the two of them came into the house. He smiled at me, saying, "Well, well, now, is that your little girl? Hello there, little girl." My mother went straight to the red sofa, reached inside the top cushion. When she turned around, there was a gun in her hand. She just stood there, her long fingers wrapped around that small dull-blue gun, both hands holding it firm and steady. The man stopped smiling and backed out the door. He never said another word. Nor did my mother.

We moved again then, away from the house with the front yard of green-tinted cement. This time we packed and moved

quickly, far away across town. My mother rented a truck
and she hired two men to load it for us. She hurried them
too. Our beds, the red velvet sofa, the two folding bridge
chairs, the refrigerator and the gas stove, the enamel-topped
kitchen table, the armoire with the cracked mirrored doors—
they fitted neatly into the truck along with the boxes of
clothes and dishes and my mother's sewing machine, which
was the only new thing we owned.

"Hurry," my mother said, carrying some of the smaller
things herself, "we haven't got all day. I am paying you to
be quick."

Grumbling and complaining, the men finished the loading
and took their money and stood on the sidewalk to watch
us leave.

"Get in," my mother said to me. "Be quick."

We drove down highways lined with withered brown palm
trees, past endless intersections where traffic lights stabbed
out their signals like lighthouses. We waited, part of an
impatient horn-blowing crowd, while canal bridges opened
to let gravel-filled barges glide past through oily water.

And my mother said nothing at all. When I could wait
no longer, when the silence between us seemed more dangerous and frightening than any nightmare, I asked, "Why
are we running away?"

"To be safe," she said.

"Is it far?"

"It is far enough to be safe," she said.

When we finally reached the place where we would live,
she hired two more neighborhood men to take our things
up the stairs. She had moved without leaving a trace behind.

I guessed it had something to do with her visitor, but I
did not worry. In all the stories my mother had told me,
there were always threats and pursuits and enemies to be

avoided. It was the way a princess lived. And my mother was always there, to bring me to safety at last.

When we sat in our new home, in the clutter of boxes and furniture, when we were safely inside, the door locked behind us, my mother smiled at me, a great slow smile that showed square strong teeth in the smooth darkness of her face. "My hidden princess," she said, "my lotus flower. . ."

The accustomed endearments tumbled from her lips, the expected exotic song of love and praise. I, young as I was, noted the change. For the past few days, and on the drive across town, she had spoken rarely, and then only in the crisp blunt language of everyday.

Now, by the smooth soft flow of her words, I knew that we were indeed safe. We had passed through a series of lodgings—I think I remember them all, even the one where I was born, the one with a chinaberry tree outside the window—but we had finally gained our castle, the one we had been searching for. There was even a turret, to command the approaches and to defend against enemies.

The house stood on a corner. Its old clapboard walls rose directly from the sidewalk through two stories of flaking gray paint to a roof decorated with fancy wooden scallops; in the dark spaces under the eaves generations of pigeons nested and fluttered. At the second-floor corner, jutting over the sidewalk, was a small turret or tower, capped with a high pointed roof like a clown's hat.

Inside the tower was a hinged seat of varnished wood entirely covered by scratch drawings: flowers and initials and hearts, dancing stick figures and even a face or two. Here we stored odd bits of things: old shoes, an umbrella with a broken rib, a doll in a pink and blue gingham dress, an Easter bunny of purple and yellow plush, a black patent purse. Roaches lived there too; they ate the stuffing from the doll and the feather from her hat, and they ate spots of fur from the Easter bunny so that it looked burned. I thought they had also nibbled the edge of the patent leather purse, but my mother said no, it was just use-worn.

Day after day, I sat on top that jumble of things, above the secret workings of insects, and I watched through the windows, three panes of glass on the three sides of my tower, which my mother washed every month, so that I might see clearly.

Most of the floor below us was occupied by a drugstore, a small dark place that smelled of disinfectant and sugar candy, of brown paper and cough medicine. On two of the other corners were small houses, one room wide, perched off the ground on low brick foundations and edged by foot-wide runners of grass. On the third corner, directly across from my window was Providence Manor, a home for the old. A tall iron fence enclosed an entire block of grass and trees and even occasional blooming flowers, a wilderness that stretched out of my sight. Just inside the fence was a gravel path where, on good days, the old people walked, some slowly on canes, some with arms flexing rapidly in a military march, some in chairs wheeled by nuns in black habits and white headdresses. They rotated past the spear points of the fence, every good day taking their quota of sun and exhaust-laden air. After dark, on rainy nights, the flashing sign in the drugstore window beat against those railings, broke and ran off down the shiny black street.

Downstairs too, directly below, in our small slice of the old house, were the two rooms that were my mother's workshop and showroom. On our front door—up two wooden steps from the uneven brick sidewalk—was a small neat sign: MODISTE. My mother had lettered that herself; she had always been very clever with her hands. It was the first real shop she had.

I spent my days either at my window or in my mother's workrooms. The rest of the house, the other two rooms, I don't remember at all. I was either a princess in my tower or a mannequin in my mother's clothes.

Not until years later did I realize that all the faces I saw were black. (To me they had no color, no color at all.) The people walking on the street, the old on their therapeutic rounds, the Sisters of the Holy Family, the drivers impatiently threading their way through the heavy street traffic, my mother and her customers—they all wore black skin.

As did the children in school. Eventually I had to go to school. My mother did not send me when I was six, as the law said she must. For one extra year I dreamed and flaunted my beautiful dresses. I doubt that the authorities would have noticed had I not gone to school at all. I think it was my mother's new friend who finally persuaded her. For my mother at last had a friend, a good friend whose visits were regular and predictable. For him my mother bathed and did her hair and cooked specially and smiled when the doorbell rang.

My mother's friend was a tall, heavy man who came to church with us every Sunday and afterwards held my hand as I walked along the top of the low wall that bordered the churchyard. He owned a small cab company—he drove one himself—whose insignia was a lightning bolt across a bright blue circle. His name was David Clark, and he took me to school and picked me up every day of my first year.

I went to parochial school. Navy skirts and white blouses and black and white saddle oxfords, all of us. All of us, rows of little black raisins, waiting to be taught to read and to count and to love Lord Jesus. But I was the only one picked up by taxi every day at three o'clock. The children stared at me as I rode away, the Indian princess in her palanquin, the treasure of the mahal above Leconte's Drugstore.

On the first day of school my mother went with me. I remember very little about that day—I was nauseated with excitement, griped with fear—but I remember the dress she wore. She had made it herself of course, just as she had made my school uniform; it was brown linen, a long-sleeved blouse and an eight-gore skirt. I saw the nuns' eyes flick over us in brief appraisal: we passed with honors. (I took it as my due. I wonder now how my mother felt.)

The school smelled of peanuts and garlic bologna. The floor of my classroom was spotted with puddles of slimy liquid. Oddly enough, the other children's panic quieted me. In the reek of their nervousness, my own stomach settled, and when the harried janitor arrived with a bucket of sawdust to sprinkle on the vomit, I helped him by pushing aside the desks.

That first day was the longest I have ever known. And the hottest. It was early September and the afternoon sun burned through the window shades to polish our faces with sweat—all except the teaching sister. Her face remained dry and dull as if coated with a film of dust.

I never grew used to the noise and rush of children leaving class. When the bell sounded, I always waited while the room emptied. Then, in a pause disturbed only by the soft sounds of the teacher gathering her papers, I walked slowly through the door, last and alone. Always alone, except for once, years later when I was at boarding school at St. Mary's, mine the only dark face in a sea of Irish skin. (The other girls simply ignored me, saw through me as if I were invisible or transparent.) By the time I had gathered my books and reached the door, their departing backs were far down the hall. But at St. Mary's I was not alone. My companion was a moonfaced child of my own age who had rheumatoid arthritis, took massive doses of cortisone, and moved with the slow painful dignity of an ancient woman. She died in our second year of high school. I, along with every other girl in the school, wrote a letter of condolence to her parents. Mine was never acknowledged.

But that was in the future, in the time when I was no longer a child, a good many years away.

For first grade, I had two skirts, made by my mother according to the uniform dress code of the parochial school system, and two blouses. Every second day, when I came home, I was expected to wash my blouse carefully, using the kitchen sink and a small scrubbing board that my mother kept underneath, propped against the pipes. I then hung it on the back porch inside the screen, where no bird could soil it. Every so often my mother was dissatisfied with its whiteness and she would wash it again in bleach. The next time I wore that blouse I was certain to have a rash across my neck and shoulders where the fabric rubbed my skin.

Later on, when my growing required new blouses (the skirts had deep hems to let down), my mother made them slightly different. She added small tucks down the front, two tiny rows on each side of the buttons. I noticed the nuns looking at me—they were very strict about uniforms in those days—and they must have written to my mother. My next blouses were perfectly plain. What the nuns couldn't know about were my slips. My mother made my slips too, and they had all the elaborate decorations that my blouses lacked. They were tucked, with drawn lace and wide bands of crochet at the shoulders, and a deep flounce of lace at the hem. Only one nun ever saw them and she wasn't really a nun. She was a novice: very young, shorter even than I was. She was cleaning the bathrooms and I, not noticing her, was fanning myself with my skirt against the heat. She stopped and fingered my slip. "What lovely work, what exquisite work." Then she looked shocked and ashamed—perhaps she had made a vow of silence—and she went hastily back to her pail and mop.

After the first year at school, I took the city bus home. The stop was at our corner. All I had to do was cross the street and open the door. Once inside, I rushed to bathe, to brush my hair, to put on the dresses that my mother would sell. Wearing her clothes and her dreams, I would move carefully among her customers, gracefully, as only a princess can.

The lotus blossom. The treasure of the mahal. In the women's faces I saw greed and covetousness. My mother's order books rustled busily. I myself drew spirit and sustenance from the flickering eyes and the fingers stretched out to touch. In the small crowded room, I had come into my castle and my kingdom.

And so I passed my childhood disguised to myself as a princess. I thrived, grew strong and resilient. When the kingdom at last fell and the castle was conquered, and I lost my crown and my birthright, when I stood naked and revealed as a young black female of illegitimate birth, it hardly mattered. By then the castle and the kingdom were within me and I carried them away.

HUNTER

As the plane began its descent into Clarksdale, Nancy Martinson stretched and sighed, closed her magazine and tucked it away neatly. Her husband and younger daughter slept soundly in the seats next to her; across the aisle her other daughter worked a crossword puzzle.

Outside the brilliant morning sunshine thinned to a yellow hazy glow. On the ground below, patches of fog shrouded the neatly plowed cornfields and clung to the brushy sides of the hills. The plane banked, circled; she saw a black strip of highway and a single car on it.

The engines slowed, changed tone, settling the plane for its final approach. With a soft hiss, the wheels went down. Thick gray fog wiped the window empty.

She sat back, rubbing her neck, dutifully checking her seat belt, waiting for the landing, watching the fog-obscured window. And saw a tree race past, leaves spattering like rain against the window.

Somebody has thrown a tree at us, she thought foolishly. How can that be.

The floor rose, lurching hard against her feet. She was shaken like a rag doll, so violently she could scarcely breathe.

She wrapped her arms around her body, holding on, while her head pounded against the seat back. Her knees jerked up, beating against her crossed arms. She heard loud squeals like tires on pavement and a steady high-pitched metallic whine. And voices, massed voices like a church choir far away. But no, she thought with sluggish wonder, those were screams.

She held tightly to herself as she careened through flashes of light and dark, through roaring oceans of sound. Shaking violently like a flag snapping in the wind.

A yellow column of flame appeared in the aisle. Glittering, shining. The color of sun, burning like sun.

She saw her daughter—recognized the blue and white stripes of her dress—saw her daughter, arms outstretched, rise to meet it. Pass through the gleaming gateway and vanish.

Next to her, her husband was rising, stretching. She saw clearly the initial on his shirt sleeve. He reached for her, missed, called to her. Before he vanished in the brilliant light.

She too would follow. . . . But the arms wrapped around her body refused to loosen their grip. Her feet stamped down against the lurching floor and found nothing there. She struggled, bent double, thrashing from side to side.

Then she was free. In silence, in complete and perfect silence, she floated slowly through air that was sprinkled and speckled with glitter. Fell forever along rainbows like giant playground slides. Ended at last with trees bending over her, surrounding her. To hold them back, she lifted her hands straight out in front of her, fingers spread.

All around her small lives went on, undisturbed. Grass broke through its softened seed, uncoiling to the surface, lifting tents of mud on the points of its sharp blades. Leaves

unrolled from their tight curls on the twigs overhead, relax-
ing to the air with soft whisperings of content.

She heard ants running across the surface of the earth, feet
clattering like iron boots. She heard grains of sand shift and
rattle within the tunnels worms dug patiently below the surface. And she saw that the ground around her spurted blood
like many fountains and the worms' tunnels flooded red.

Sam Flanders, in his second year with KLR-News, left his
apartment half an hour early for work. He checked his watch,
then checked again with the car radio. He shrugged: thirty
minutes' lost sleep. Well, since he had extra time, he wouldn't
fight interstate traffic. He'd go the long way, by back roads,
through the country.

He drove out Perkins Road, past miles of new yellow-
green cornfields, hazy with night fog. He turned down
Bingham Lane, a small blacktopped road that ran through
old pasture fields just west of the airport. By night this stretch
of road was the most popular lovers' lane in the county.
There were car tracks running into the brush on both sides
and piles of beer cans and bottles half covered by Johnson
grass.

Maybe there was a story in that, he thought automatically, absentmindedly: Alcohol and Youth. The news director was a prohibitionist at heart; maybe he'd go for something
like that.

He slowed in a heavy patch of fog and then moments
later rose into bright sun at the top of a hill. The fog was
always bad out here. It would burn itself off in strips and
shreds and the area wouldn't be clear until nearly noon.
He thought: They build airports in these low waste areas

and then wonder why they have so many instrument approaches.

Back into the fog. He turned on his headlights and started the windshield wipers. Nothing to do but creep along.

Because the windows were closed against the morning chill, he heard the impact as a dull thud. He blinked, uncertain, seeing nothing. Another muffled sound. He opened the window and leaned out into the wet air. A couple of loud pops: he wasn't sure of their direction.

The fog seemed thicker than ever. He turned on his car's emergency flashers and drove with his head half out the open window. Nothing. He pulled off the road and got out: still nothing. He hesitated; there was a faint smell of something in the air and the fog itself seemed to tremble and dance. A few spatters of rain splashed his face.

He drove on again, puzzled and curious. A mile farther and he noticed a faint glow to his right, the fog darkened suddenly and he smelled oily smoke.

He held his breath and blinked rapidly. His jaw quivered, he stopped it with his hand. He glanced at his watch without actually seeing it. Then, carefully, methodically, he let the words form in his mind: an incoming flight has crashed short of the runway.

His eyes still on the distant glow, he reached for the radio to call his office. He was precise and slow: ". . . Near the north end of Bingham Lane, visible from the road. Would you repeat that to me?" The electronic voice cackled it back to him. "Right. You got it. I'm going over there now."

It was farther than he thought, much farther. His run slowed to a trot as he made his way along a series of gullies, stumbling, sliding on the wet leaf mold, splashing through green-skimmed pools. When the overhead mist gleamed bright yellow and drops of fog sparkled like points of ice, he left the gully and began climbing a steep pine hill. His leather shoes slipped on the needle-covered ground, he grabbed trunks and branches to pull himself crosswise up the slope. There was an overhang at the top, soft and yielding. He scrambled across.

From here he looked directly down at the broken fuselage and the towering feather of black smoke, flame-edged.

He shivered in the gleaming heat, his knees buckled and he crouched animal-fashion on the ground. The flames seemed to reach to him, to beckon him. And he heard clearly: pealing bells, bells of jubilation.

In panic he rolled and stumbled back down the slope, to hide in the thickest pines. To wait for the fire trucks and the company of other live men.

By the time the first emergency vehicles arrived and the crews filled the air with their shouts, he'd noticed something a couple of hundred yards away through the thin bare trunks: a bright spot. He climbed toward it, moving slowly, gingerly, as if the ground might explode with his weight. He found an airplane seat wedged into the soft earth of a small rainwash. And in the seat a woman in a pale yellow dress. She lay on her back, arms stretched out, palms up. Her face was blackened and there were large smudges across her dress; her shoeless feet hung limply, toes down. She was so still he thought she was dead, until her wide-open eyes blinked, very slowly. He moved closer and saw the tiny rhythmical movement of small shallow breaths.

Overhead a mockingbird chattered and began to sing. Sam Flanders scrambled toward the top of the ridge, shouting for help.

———

For Nancy Martinson time came and went in a pattern of overhead fluorescent tubes, crisscrossed by faces. Some white, some dark, some blood red. Some with glasses circling their eyes. Some bearded like pirates. Some wearing white sails on their heads, set to drive them on the wind. (She heard the wind whistling and the steady clank of buoys and the sound of surf. What shore was that?)

The faces bobbed across the fluorescent-streaked sky like balloons on a string. Their hands were hooks, they propped her up, put food into her mouth, massaged her jaws and stroked her throat, and dragged her stumbling up and down closed tubes of space.

They began speaking to her. A full-rigged sailing ship said, "Nancy, Nancy, can you hear me?"

The sails sped off into the distance and became a small triangle of starched cap. "Do I know you?" she said politely.

Under the cap was a round face with dark eyebrows graying like frost. "Dr. Thigpen will be so delighted. Everybody will be so delighted."

"Why will they be delighted? Who are they to be delighted?"

The round face smiled a gentle doll's smile. And the porcelain smile hardened and froze.

Eventually another smile hung in its place. Then another. There was never a moment when a shiny polished face was not watching and smiling.

Sometimes she spoke to them and sometimes she didn't. She discovered bit by bit they were real, that they smelt of perspiration and perfume and tobacco.

She learned that they all wanted to talk to her. Carefully, so very carefully, so slowly.

Do you know who you are? they wanted to know. And when were you born? And when did you marry?

She grew irritated at their childish probing and refused to answer, saying: I have never heard anything so silly.

They looked confused and a little hurt, so she changed her mind and said only: Don't ask such stupid questions. I'm not feebleminded.

Do you know what has happened? they asked. Yes, she said, the plane crashed. There were trees banging against the window. Like people wanting to get in.

Dr. Thigpen—he came very often, he had thick gray hair and the long sad face of an old horse—said, "Do you remember that your husband and your two daughters were on that plane with you?"

"Yes," she said and then: "You've changed the questions. Before you would say: Was there anybody on the plane with you. Perhaps you think I don't remember, but I do."

"It was my mistake," he said.

"I don't think so," she said.

He continued as if he hadn't heard: "They were on the plane with you."

"I will tell you what you want to know," she said, "or what I think you want to know. I know who I am and I know that I am in a hospital, though I don't know exactly where. I know that my husband and my two daughters, whose names are Anna and Marsha, were killed. I saw them die. I saw the whole plane die."

"Yes." He polished his glasses, replaced them. She read in his eyes uncertainty and calculation. "You were thrown free, some hundred feet, they tell me, and down a very steep slope. Do you remember anything of that?"

"There were mockingbirds singing," she said, "and a wind blowing."

"Other people, the rescue crews, remember birds singing," he said.

She shrugged; other people were nothing to her.

"The wind of course was the flames. Do you remember anything more, how you got there?"

"I fell out," she said. "I slipped right out between one second and the next—there was a little hesitation, a little opening, and I fell through."

The thought in his eyes ended, like doors closing. "There'll be a formal hearing, there always is, they tell me. Normally you might be asked to testify. But under the circumstances I'm going to recommend very strongly that you not be contacted in any way."

She shrugged. "It is nothing to me whether I talk to them or to you or to any other of God's creatures."

An appraising look from the glasses. "Do you know you were the only one to survive?"

Again she saw the pillar of flame, tattered streamers flying. She saw it sweep down the aisle, gleaming.

Survive. She looked into his two shiny rounds of eyeglass held together by a strip of gold. No, I didn't, she said silently. No, I didn't.

Now Nancy Martinson sat by a window and watched a flat expanse of rooftops sprinkled with trees and speared by telephone poles. In the distance there was a bridge with traffic moving slowly across it, at night the cars became fireflies crawling up her windowpane. She listened: horns and sirens, urgent, complaining, angry; mumbling engines and tires hissing on asphalt; coughs and shouts and mutters and curses; dogs barking and babies crying and the soft singsong of cats on the prowl.

Her brother Stephen came, and his wife, Lois. Nancy watched their tears and wondered if their grief would add appreciably to the general noise level outside in the world.

"There's nothing I can say, Nancy, what can I say?"

Lois sobbed and choked and ran from the room. They could hear her heels down the corridor, getting smaller and smaller, until they sounded like a distant woodpecker.

"It was an accident," Nancy said.

"But, my God!"

"Accidents happen," Nancy told him, explaining slowly, carefully. "According to the laws of probability, a predictable number of people die in a predictable number of ways during any given time period."

He stared at her, silent, tears making shiny smears on his cheeks.

"Airline fatalities are one for each eight million passenger miles."

A tear reached his lip, his tongue hesitantly licked it away.

"Robert and I looked that up once."

He dried his cheek with his fingers. "Poor Robert."

"We decided we would fly together, the whole family. So no one would survive alone.... Do you remember when we were little, Stephen, we'd pull the tails off lizards, they'd run off, and the tails would be left behind, jerking and twitching.... Do you remember when we played under the chinaberry tree by the swing?" Sweet pale purple flowers and thousands of seeds on the ground. "We'd play marbles with the seeds," she said.... Those houses she saw from her window, they must have chinaberry trees, and children playing under them. She could still feel the dry sandy soil between her fingers.

"Will you live with us now?" her brother asked.

"No, of course not."

Dr. Thigpen came in the room. "You move so silently," she said. "Are all psychiatrists so quiet? I've never had to do with one before."

"I wear rubber-soled shoes." His smile flashed on, then settled to a half-speed glow.

"I'll go home now," she said. "To my house."

Dr. Thigpen nodded. "Your brother will see that everything is taken care of for you."

"Yes," said Stephen eagerly. "Anytime you want to go home, we'll drive you. I know you don't want to fly. . . ."

How silly he was, she thought. Even as a child, she hadn't liked him very much. "Of course I'll fly. I'll have to fly a great deal now. It will be tiresome, but I'll have to."

In the months that followed Sam Flanders worked unusually hard. He got a job offer and a raise to stay where he was. He did some good stories: a holdup at the National Bank of Commerce on Main Street; financial irregularities in the food stamp program; an explosion in a grain elevator. And he wanted to do a follow-up on the crash survivor.

"Jesus," the news director said. "You know better than that. We didn't do a story on the hearings because nobody wants to think about pilot error. And that woman doesn't even live in town."

"Okay," Sam said. "Okay." He put the woman's name and address in his desk. "I'll forget it."

But the images wouldn't go away, they seemed to get

brighter and clearer. When he'd looked straight into the fire, and he'd heard bells like Easter bells in Rome . . . And the mockingbirds singing so close to the wreck . . . He'd wake up at night hearing those birds.

He decided to look for upbeat stories. He did one about drug rehabilitation through diet and exercise. He interviewed a prostitute who'd found salvation in Charismatic Catholicism. He did a two-part story on the Animal Rescue League and adopted a large fuzzy Samoyed.

He decided that he wanted to marry his girl friend at the same time she decided she didn't want to marry anybody. He bought a pure-bred Siamese, found that it didn't get on with the Samoyed, and gave the cat to his mother. He joined a health club and played racquet ball almost every evening. He went to his sister's wedding and signed the register with a great flourish. He even planned his vacation six months ahead: he decided he would go to Aspen.

And still that woman would not leave him alone. Almost every night, just the other side of sleep, she waited for him.

Just as he'd first found her: tossed against a curl of mud bank. Safe as Moses in the bullrushes. Arms holding up the sky.

At two thirty one morning Sam Flanders made up his mind. He would call her, and he would go see her, if she would let him.

He fell asleep then, dreamless heavy sleep, didn't hear his alarm clock, and was almost an hour late for work.

Nancy Martinson came home from her regular eleven o'clock appointment at the Royal Beauty Salon to find Sam Flanders waiting, his car parked at the curb.

"Oh dear," she said, "I'd forgotten you. You're that young man from Clarksdale."

She shook hands quickly and firmly; beauty shop scents of shampoo and hair spray swirled in the air. "Do you know you're the first person to mention the accident to me since I left the hospital."

"If you could give me just a few minutes."

"That's about all I've got, I have a two o'clock flight. But come in."

"Yes, ma'am," he said.

"Will you have a drink?" A polite lift of eyebrows. "I only have Scotch—that's what I drink—I so rarely have company."

"If you're having one, I will too."

"On the porch," she said. "I always have my lunchtime drink out there."

The porch was glass-enclosed and comfortable, all white wicker and striped canvas cushions.

"Robert always came home for lunch," she said. "That's one of the advantages of a small town. We would have a drink out here. Even in winter, even when it was snowing, he liked this porch."

On the low table there was a bottle of Scotch, ice, two small bottles of soda, and two glasses.

Two glasses, he thought, two. So she hadn't forgotten him. . . .

She said, as if she'd heard his thought, "No, I really had forgotten you. Elizabeth leaves the bar things here before she goes home, just the way she's done for the last eight years." A pause so long that he lifted his head. She smiled vaguely. "It has been a while since anyone used Robert's glass."

She fixed his Scotch and soda quickly, handed it to him

with a linen napkin tucked neatly beneath, then poured hers on the rocks. "Do you know, for a while when I first came back, after the accident, I would pour Robert's drink and then I would sit here and wait for him to come in." She smiled gently, self-deprecatingly. "I thought somehow that if I arranged things the way they used to be, I could compel Robert to come back." Again a shrug. "Is that drink all right?"

"Yes, ma'am, it's fine. I was just admiring your garden."

"Robert liked it so very much. You know, Mr. Flanders, you can't do a story. I don't want any publicity, none at all. I didn't think of that when I talked to you, or I could have saved you the trouble of driving all the way here."

"My station doesn't want to do a story. That isn't why I came. I just wanted to see, well, how things had come out." His words sounded silly. And his Scotch and soda tasted very strange.

She listened politely, faintly puzzled, not very interested.

"You see, I was the first person to reach the plane."

He had expected some reaction from her—surprise or disgust or anger. But she did not react at all. She went on patiently waiting, sipping her drink.

He took a deep breath and tried again. "I was the one to find you."

"I don't remember," she said.

"Nobody expects you to, I guess. But still I thought you might."

"No."

"I came to the hospital but they said no visitors, and I didn't want to intrude on you here at home."

"Until now."

"Until now when I had a special reason." How could he tell her that he'd come because she haunted his dreams and kept him awake at night.

The telephone rang. He jumped, the ice rattled in his glass. "Is the bell too loud?" she said. There was a wall phone behind her; she answered it while he stirred his drink with one finger.

"No," she said crisply, "no, I'm not coming in next week. I'm sure I told you." She listened, one hand absentmindedly patting her hair. "I explained it all to the doctor. . . . No, no matter who pays for it . . . It's a waste of time." She laughed out loud, a startling girlish sound. "He thinks I *should* . . . how silly. Now, please, I'm busy and I haven't time to argue."

She sat down, the pleats of her navy skirt falling neatly and precisely to each side. "That's rather amusing. My psychiatrist thinks I should continue treatment. . . . Have you ever been? No? A very strange treatment, talking and talking."

"I've heard it's very expensive." Thinking: That was a different woman on the phone, firm, steady, no nervous flutters or forgetfulness.

"They thought it was a matter of money, too. So they reminded me that the insurance would continue paying the bill. Rehabilitation, so to speak."

"Of course." This was a good beginning. Nothing like dollars and cents to settle people down.

"They decided that if I wasn't hurt physically I had to be injured mentally." She smiled pleasantly. Just a trace of fluttery vagueness now.

"Were you?" Too abrupt. Careful, he thought.

"No," she said quietly.

"I read somewhere that common carriers are liable for their passengers' safety."

"I suppose so." She did not sound interested. "My brother Stephen took care of that. It does seem to be quite simple. A price list, really. How much a person is worth, up to a limit of some sort. I don't exactly know how, but it seems that everyone pretty much agrees how it's got to be done."

A price list. Her choice of words disturbed him. He took another sip of his drink. Awful. And then he saw the label on the small soda bottle: TONIC. He was drinking Scotch and tonic. . . . He wondered whether to tell her and decided not to.

The phone rang again. "Yes, Stephen, I'm just about to leave for the airport. Yes, in a very few minutes. Just as soon as Mr.—What was your name? . . . Flanders—leaves. No, you don't want to talk to him. Really, Stephen, you do get so excited. Yes, of course. Good-bye, Stephen."

A quiet return to her seat. "He is a nice man, my brother. He hates to see me disturbed." She smiled, waiting for him to speak.

Sam Flanders said, "I'm a little surprised that you're still flying, and so casually. I imagined you'd think more about it."

Her eyes were a deep blue, shiny as tears, but there were no tears there. "I have to fly. And I do think a great deal about it." Abruptly the bright blue eyes lost their glitter. They grew dull and slate-colored and flat as frozen pond ice. "I will tell you," she said, "but I wonder if you will understand."

He took a short breath; you'd think he was afraid. "I could try. If you could tell me."

"When the plane crashed, a flame came down the aisle, a pillar of flame; no, not even that, it didn't have a real shape. It was just a light in the center of the plane and people were reaching for it, to touch it. And then there was a pause."

She looked at him. "I've thought about ways to explain it to other people, to myself too. It was like there was a drum, beating very fast, very even, without emphasis. Then one of those beats was missing. Sometimes I imagine it written on a sheet of music, that one missing beat."

"Yes," he said, "yes."

"And I was tossed out, right there."

She nodded to herself, emphatically. "I should have died, you see."

He was beginning to believe her. He was beginning to be as crazy as she was. No wonder the psychiatrist wanted her to stay in treatment.

"There was no way I could have survived," she said flatly. "Everybody told me that."

That was true, he thought. She was alive, and she ought not be.

"At first—in the hospital—I thought I was dead. I expected to fall down any minute. I thought there was just some sort of delay, a temporary suspension.

"But it wasn't that."

Her eyes had the funny color of newborn babies', the no-color of darkness.

"When I kept on living, then I began to understand."

"What?" he said. "What?"

Now she spoke rapidly and mechanically, as if she'd thought about this so often it no longer interested her, it was just a fact learned and repeated like a child's multiplication tables. "Time is smooth and steady. Usually, that's the way it is, but not always. There are flaws in everything, even time. I fell through one and was left behind."

He sat silent, watching the blue color return to her large round eyes.

"You know," she said, "I think you believe me."

"You know," he said, "I think I do."

She smiled at him, kindly, maternal. "We can have one more drink and then I must get to the airport."

Automatically he took the drink, sipped. The peaty taste of good heavy Scotch filled his mouth. He glanced at the bottle: soda this time. He took a few comforting swallows. "Why do you say you have to fly?"

"You can't get beyond the fact that I came back to this house without a scratch on me," she said soothingly. "That's very misleading, you know. I died on that plane, I'm just not dead. I was supposed to be with my family. Now I have to go back and catch up with them. They'll be expecting me, they'll be wondering where I am.... Do you go to church?"

"No, ma'am," he said.

"I used to go before, but I haven't since."

"Did you think of killing yourself?" He regretted saying it, he wouldn't want to give her ideas.

"Yes, of course. I have a bottle of Seconal just for the purpose. But that wouldn't work."

"It wouldn't?"

"Then I'd be lost and without them forever. You'll understand if you give yourself time to think about it." The round blue eyes urged him to try. "I have to find the right spot to enter."

She wiped the condensation off her glass. "They'll wait for me, they'll know I'm looking for the way. And one day I'll find it. Do you see?"

He shook his head.

She took a deep patient breath. "There are airline fatalities, predictable ones. Inexorable. Unchangeable. So I fly."

He put his drink down abruptly. "You're looking for a crash."

"I was almost on that plane in Chicago a few months ago ... I fly constantly. It's about the only way I have to spend my money."

"But the other people," he said. "Don't you ever think you're killing the other people?"

She laughed, clearly, brightly. "No, I don't think I'm bad luck, or anything so ridiculous. If anyone dies, it's chance. It's not because of me."

"But you're looking forward to it."

"Yes." She spread her fingers, studying her fresh manicure. "Yes. With each and every flight."

"I believe you," he said.

"And now I really must go, or I'll miss my connections. This is going to be such a busy trip. First I go to Denver, then St. Louis. I spend the night there and go on to San Francisco, and Los Angeles and San Diego. The following day I go to Phoenix and Midland and New Orleans. And then—I'm not sure where I spend the night—I go to Miami and Jacksonville and Atlanta and Louisville, then Washington, New York, Boston, and back home."

She would have covered the country, he thought. "Looking," he said aloud.

She patted his arm. "I thought you'd understand. I suppose it has to do with your being there.... You were out of time too, weren't you? You don't ordinarily drive by the airport?"

"No, ma'am," he said. "That wasn't my regular way to work."

"You see? These little irregularities happen all the time. Mostly they're like a stumble and you pick yourself up and you're fine. It's not often serious."

Her bags were in the hall, packed and waiting. He put them in her car. "Good-bye," he said. "Maybe you'll find it, you know. What you're looking for."

"Oh yes," she said, "I'm quite certain. On one of those planes, I'll find it. Good-bye, Mr. Flanders." She was radiantly happy, a perfect bride on the morning of her wedding.

Jesus, he thought, she is crazy, out of it, spaced ...

"There's just one thing, Mr. Flanders. And I've been wondering if I should say this, but are you all right?"

"Yes," he said, "I'm fine."

"Are you sure? That first Scotch was made with tonic—Elizabeth put out the wrong bottle again. You couldn't have liked it, could you?"

"I must not have noticed." So who was crazy? Why hadn't he said anything? Why had he drunk the damn stuff?

She began to giggle, hesitated, then laughed out loud.

He tried to look offended, gave up, and laughed with her.

For a few seconds their voices shook the nearest rose petals and raced out across the leaves to spend themselves against the closed and locked house door.

She finished, sighed, nodded to him and drove away. In the silence, the startled birds began to sing again.

Nancy Martinson watched him in her rearview mirror. He stood for a moment, flicked his fingers at the nearest rosebush, then got into his car.

He seemed a nice young man, she thought. And really quite handsome.

She glanced in the mirror again. His car was pulling out of the driveway.

Just the sort of young man her daughters would have dated. The sort of son-in-law she would have had. She would have liked grandchildren. It must be very pleasant to think of your blood continuing in an endless link to the future.

Still, it wasn't so bad for her, she thought. Her life was

more than half lived. But it was terrible, dreadful about the
girls. They'd had so little time.

When they met, she'd tell them about that young man.
But then, perhaps not. It might be best for her to say nothing at all.

That young man would have beautiful children one day.
They just wouldn't be hers.

She reached the stop sign at Cobbs Hill Road. As always
her heart began to sing with joy and expectation and secret
knowledge: Maybe this time. She was getting so tired. It
was taking so very long. Still, maybe now. She smiled at
the sky and the trees, at the neat flower gardens, at everything. And she turned down the road to the airport.

She glanced once more in the mirror. The road behind
her was empty. The young man had gone the other way.

LETTING GO

As Free{ing persons, recollect the Snow—
First—Chill—then Stupor—then the letting go—

EMILY DICKINSON

Except for a couple of cruising sea gulls, the entire north shore of the bay was empty and still—the tumbled concrete blocks of the erosion barriers, the wide mud flats, ripple-covered now by high tide. Far offshore, a mile or so, the silver gray water darkened into the slate gray of the deep buoy-marked ship channel where oil tankers passed in slow procession against an always hazy horizon.

Mary Margaret knew every line and shadow out there. She'd grown up watching—sitting on the front porch in summer, and in winter rubbing a little frost-free spot on the windowpane. She'd wished for a ship to come sailing right up to the shore, a pirate ship with blood red sails and a big black flag. Or a white and gold yacht, its crew dressed in navy and braid. But this part of the bay was only a few feet deep, and good for nothing but summer fishermen. Their outboards left shimmering oil stains on the quiet surface and their beer cans drifted to the beach and caught in the break-water.

She sniffed the familiar decaying smell of salt shore as she parked in front of her parents' house and checked her watch. Right on time. They were expecting her, they knew she was always prompt. But no front curtain moved, no front door opened. The house looked as it always did—small, gray, like a nun with folded hands, waiting or sleeping.

She thought: Just once they might be looking for me. I come every Wednesday for supper and the novena. Perpetual novena. That was how I learned what eternity was— like the novena, it goes on and on without end.

She climbed the narrow concrete driveway, barely wide enough for a car, cut deep into the slope, terraced carefully and secured by creeping greenery, perfectly clipped. All as neat as an ironed handkerchief.

Now three concrete steps up to the walk. The lawn was still green, there'd been no frosts, and the yellow mums were full and glowing in their beds. There were even a few dozen pink roses on the climber against the house.

It was a marvel, this garden. Her parents' pride. Since his retirement, her father spent his days out here, working until the hard winter freezes forced him inside and returning with the first feel of spring in the air, brushing aside the last melting patches of snow.

They take more care of the garden, she thought, than they ever did of me.

That goddamned garden, Edward called it. In the first months of their marriage, when Edward tried very hard to be friendly with her parents, he'd sent them a present, a special lightweight battery-powered weed trimmer. "It's for their goddamn garden," he said. "Even if they can't stand me, they got to like this." He'd been wrong.

Her parents had never used the trimmer. They hadn't even given it to one of the parish fairs at St. Joseph's Church.

They had simply thrown it out. When Mary Margaret and Edward came for dinner the following Wednesday, they found the trimmer, unopened in its bright red and yellow carton, lying across the trash cans at curbside.

Collection wasn't until Monday, Mary Margaret thought dully. Her parents weren't just throwing away an unwanted present. They had intended only one thing—for Edward to see it. . . . He picked up the trimmer, holding it delicately as china, turning it, examining it carefully. He brushed off a few bits of grass before putting it in the trunk of their car.

"I am not going in there," he said quietly to Mary Margaret. "Will you come home with me or will you go on?"

She didn't answer. She couldn't. She fumbled for words and found none.

He nodded. "I've had enough. I am not going into that house again, and I am not going to see them again, not even at their funerals. I will come back and pick you up whatever time you say. Next week you can have the car and come by yourself."

So it was settled. If her parents noticed his absence, they never mentioned it. It was as if he had never existed.

Now on another Wednesday evening, she bent to examine the dahlias, their heavy burgundy heads staked against the wind. Her father had a hand with dahlias, they were always magnificent. The red and yellow combination—dahlias and mums—was her mother's choice, repeated year after year.

And that was another thing, a strange thing. Her parents always agreed.

Everything was settled with a flick of an eye, a shrug of the shoulder—never an argument. Together they moved smoothly and silently through their days, as if they had taken a train and knew precisely where the track led.

Mary Margaret pushed open the door (her parents kept it unlocked until they went to bed) and stepped into the dim living room.

It had been brighter when she was a child, when the print curtains and the chair covers were new. Over the years darkening wood-paneled walls had absorbed their colors and turned everything into a very dense forest shade.

She'd thought of that image, years ago, when she was in high school. It still pleased her: forest shade. Not gloomy. But the regal dimness of a great forest . . .

As always her parents sat at the table by the window. Cards were neatly stacked in the very center of the table, but they weren't playing. They never played this time of day—only in the evenings for an hour or so before bed. (Her mother always used the bathroom first, while her father riffled the cards through a game of solitaire.)

Her mother was sewing—a long white piece of cloth stretched across her lap to fall in soft folds on the floor. The Altar Society. Again. How many altar cloths had her mother made over the years? And how could a church wear out so many linens?

Pencil in hand, her father was studying the *Daily Racing Form*. Soon he would carefully reconsider his findings, write down his conclusions, and phone his bookie. He was a good handicapper and a very lucky one; he won forty or fifty dollars a week. Steadily, week after week. He rarely went to the track. He didn't like crowds, he said, and all those mutuel windows were a temptation to bet too much. He liked things just the way they were. His winnings took them to dinner and a movie once a week. Which was more than his pension would ever have done.

"Hello," Mary Margaret said.

"You're here," her mother said.

Her father waved the tip of his pencil at her and went on reading.

Mary Margaret slipped off her coat.

"You didn't need that," her mother said. "It's not cold yet."

"It might be by the time I drive home."

"Not this time of year."

She folded the coat carefully on the corner of the couch. She put her purse on the coffee table, next to her father's World War II helmet with the gaping hole in its top. *Looks like some kind of can opener, huh?* he'd say now and then. *Never even parted my hair, can you believe it?* The same blast left a load of shrapnel in his back. *They missed killing me, but they sure fixed my ass,* he'd say.

For years little metal pieces worked their way out, and he'd been in the Veterans Hospital half a dozen times. There hadn't been any trouble for years now; the bits of metal and dirt must be gone at last. Still, whenever the weather was warm, he'd scratch at the long bluish-purple scars criss-crossing the backs of his thighs. They'd never quite healed.

Mary Margaret picked up the shattered helmet, now rusting ever so faintly, and fingered the ragged edges, thinking: Funny thing, luck and the difference between living and dying.

Her mother's first husband was in that same infantry company. His name was George Maley; his picture, smiling, uniformed, cap at an angle, hung on the dining room wall, all that was left of his life wrapped around by a fancy gold frame. PFC Maley had been standing next to PFC Borges when German shells began falling. . . . George Patrick Maley died (atomized, blown into dust, returned to earth with a speed greater than the grave's), and Alwyn Peter Borges lived and married his buddy's widow and sired a child.

If he'd lived, I'd be Mary Margaret Maley. I'd have different blood but the same name because my mother always planned to call her daughter Mary Margaret after her own mother.

When she was very little, long before she went to school, she used to imagine herself Mary Margaret Maley. And that the man in the picture, tall, thin, dark-haired, wide-eyed, handsome, eternally young, was her real father. Even though she knew it wasn't so.

Her father stood up very slowly, belt buckle catching the edge of the table and shaking it. He made a final check of the *Racing Form,* nodded to himself, and went to phone the bookie. The floorboards creaked under his feet.

Mary Margaret sat down next to her mother. "Another altar cloth?"

Her mother nodded. "There's only twenty members in the Altar Society and most of them don't do anything."

"People have a lot to do, they don't have the extra time."

"Last Sunday there wasn't a single bunch of flowers on the altar, not one on the main altar."

"Ma, you could have brought flowers. The garden's full of them."

Her mother stopped the methodical drawing and tying of threads. "I don't bring flowers," she said flatly.

In the long silence that followed, Mary Margaret thought: That is perfectly true. You sew, you have for years, you

will sew your way into heaven, faithful servant of Jesus. But
you have a limit. God can have the linen, but the garden
belongs to you and my father.

"I don't even have flowers in the house," her mother said,
head bent to the drawnwork again.

That was also true. The flowers stayed on bush or vine or
plant, stayed through their cycle of days and development,
withered and died. And were immediately clipped and carried away.

Her father came back, floor timbers groaning again. "I got
to put another support in that cellar," he said.

"Or go on a diet."

"Two forty. Not all that much."

"Wait till you can't bend over in the garden any more."

"I can bend over plenty good." He showed her. He could
touch his ankles with ease. "Not too bad for an old man."
He sat down again, scratching at the scars on the backs of
his thighs.

"You want some tea?" her mother asked.

"Sure," she said. "What have you got. Iced or hot?"

"Iced this time of year. It's nowhere near cold yet."

"And I didn't have to wear my coat, huh?" Mary Margaret called after her.

"She don't like to think winter's coming," her father said.
"She stands out in the yard and she don't see any signs in
the leaves."

"I don't much like it either."

"My luck's better in winter," he said. "A lot better. Why
do you suppose that is?"

There were long pauses now. Mary Margaret could feel
herself slowing down, fitting into the pace of this house. At
work she was efficient and quick and bustling, heels rattling
on the office floors. She drove the highways like a racer,

changing lanes, brake lights flashing, impatient, restless. In this house, she found silences appearing between her words, comfortable silences, like soft beds to rest your thoughts on.

"Florida," he said. "I do great at Calder. And Louisiana."

"I don't know why, Pa."

Her mother came back with three glasses of iced tea rattling on the metal tray. "No lemon this week. Said it was the truck strike or something like that."

"It's okay, Ma. I don't really care about the lemon."

"You always take lemon." Her mother picked up her work again.

Her father twirled the ice in his glass. His nails were dirt-rimmed, he never was able to scrub them clean. "Yeah," he said. "All my luck's in the south. Like the day at Gulfstream when they disqualify the winner and they hand me thirty-eight dollars and forty cents. You remember that, honey?"

Her mother's name was Christine, but he never called her that. Always honey. Maybe it had something to do with the long dead husband and friend, George Maley.

Her mother nodded absentmindedly, counting her threads. A faint odor of cooking drifted into the room. She had turned on the oven while making the tea. Tuna fish casserole. They always had tuna fish casserole before the novena on Wednesdays.

"I like those southern tracks. None of that skidding around on the ice like at Aqueduct."

She drank her iced tea slowly. Her mother had added orange juice in place of the missing lemon.

"Sometimes my luck's rotten though. Like Amato turning mule on me."

That caught her attention. "I didn't know that, Pa."

"He muled. Owed me a hundred and ninety-four dollars."

She clucked with surprise. "You don't bet that much."

He shook his head, sadly. "My best week ever. Jesus, the prices. I don't even want to think about it."

"What happened to him? Amato?"

"I don't know. I don't have nothing to do with him any more."

He is not even curious, Mary Margaret thought. The bookie he used for twenty years doesn't pay off, and he doesn't wonder what happened to him.

"When was that?" Mary Margaret said. "You didn't tell me about it."

He drank his iced tea, wiped his mouth with one finger. "Years ago. The Slob was still coming here then."

"Him," her mother echoed.

She felt the usual anger grow and turn to sharp stomachache. Him. Or the Slob. They never used his name, as if he didn't have one. Edward MacIntyre. Her husband by the rites of the Catholic Church.

"I guess there wouldn't have been time to tell me," she said, keeping her voice perfectly even. "Not when every Wednesday was a fight."

She was the one arguing, defending, pleading. Edward said nothing, only played with the food on his plate until it was time for the novena and the silence it brought.

Evenings driving home they hardly said a word, each fearful of the other's misery.

Mary Margaret said: "He came because you were my parents and I wanted him to come."

Her mother smiled patiently at her. Her father drank the last of his tea.

"You want some more tea, Al?" her mother asked.

They hadn't even come to her wedding. She'd hoped they would, until the last minute she'd hoped, right up to the minute Father Robichaux began the ceremony. Edward's parents were there, and his two brothers and their wives, and his sister and her husband and their grown son, and his unmarried sister who'd flown from Milwaukee especially for the ceremony.

In the rectory parlor that afternoon there hadn't been a single person of her blood.

I minded that most, she thought.

Stirring restlessly in her chair, Mary Margaret said, "You know, I never knew why you called him the Slob."

(She felt disloyal saying the word aloud.)

Her father laughed, her mother chuckled. Her father said, "The way he just sat there, mealy-mouthed, like he was ready to cry. He just plain looked like a slob."

Oh, she thought wearily, oh oh oh oh.

"We didn't care about him one way or the other," her mother said. Which was a very long speech for her.

And me, Mary Margaret thought, did you care nothing for me? You're my parents and you raised me and you sent me to school and you bought my clothes and took me to catechism classes. But there's got to be more than that.

"You want to watch the evening news?" she asked, abruptly changing the subject.

"Enough news in the paper," her father said.

So she crossed the room and watched by herself.

"If you gotta watch, keep it low," her father said.

She watched the flickering images, conscious now of something happening within her, of a pain that was not quite that, of a loneliness that was near to happiness.

She was not used to thinking about her feelings. They were just there, they were part of things. No more to be studied than the sky when it rained or the wind when it blew. If you worked hard and were good, there'd be nothing to trouble your thoughts.

But that didn't seem to be so.

Lately she'd started thinking about herself, she could even see so clearly. . . . The small child: black plaits down her back and skinny legs covered with half-healed scabs. The older child: the plaits crisscrossed on top her head, the scarred knees covered by longer skirts. Her Communion: white dress and veil and a crown of white flowers on the thick coil of hair. Then her hair was short and curly and there were boys and movies and high school and her first paycheck and the first clothes she had ever bought without her mother's help. Then she was nineteen and finished business school and a full-time employee of the Consolidated Service Company. She was neat and reliable and worked very hard to increase the speed and accuracy of her typing and shorthand. (She practiced every evening at home, after supper, dating only on Friday and Saturday.) She was careful to learn everybody's name and to be smiling and deferential and never never gossip. By the time she was twenty-three she was secretary to the senior vice-president. Soon she would have a fancy title like Executive Assistant and a very nice salary and she would really be somebody. When she was twenty-four she married Edward MacIntyre. He was twenty-eight, a CPA who worked in the same building. They met in line at the building's cafeteria, and they married a few months later.

They drove to work together and parted in the elevator with a kiss. In a few years they'd buy a house and later she'd take leave for a child or two and maybe even give up full-time work. For now they had a two-room apartment that was all yellow and white and green with heavy curtains to pull tight across the windows at night. She vacuumed twice a week and polished the furniture so often that the rooms always smelled of wax. She even washed the windows once a month. It was a way of quieting the restlessness that surged up in her now and then.

On Saturdays she and Edward shopped and went to a late afternoon movie, had supper at a fast-food place, and came home to bed. On Sundays in summer they went to the beach, though they didn't swim. In winter they drove out into the country where the snow was white and untouched. They never skied or skated. They were content to look at the immense shivering whiteness. And once every couple of months they got up in time to go to mass. Neither of them liked the English service, so they looked for a church where mass was still in Latin, but they found only a small group of Charismatics, and after that they'd stopped looking.

Five years.

Then two months ago, on a Thursday, Edward went home early, saying he had a headache.

She thought nothing of it. He'd looked a bit tired that morning, and there was absolutely no sense trying to work if you weren't able to do a good job.

When she got home, he was sitting in the living room. There were no lights, no lights at all, and evening dark filled the room, obscuring the leaf patterns on the chairs, dulling the white walls.

"Are you all right?" With the first jolt of alarm, she switched on one lamp. "Are you sick?"

"No," he said, "I wanted to think."

She hung up her coat, brushed it quickly, put it away neatly.

"About what?"

His dark brown eyes were flecked with yellow, they glittered like fancy marbles. Huge eyes with dark circles under them. "The way it is with us, I've been thinking, is that all there is?"

She stared at him, not answering.

"You've been feeling it too, Mary Margaret. I know that."

Carefully, levelly, without a shade of anger or fear—words to meet his words, thoughts to be born of them. No midwife here, take care. "Maybe I do wonder. Sometimes. And I don't know why."

He sat down, then got right up again. "It's hard to talk about it sensibly, you know. People go to psychiatrists for this, to find out how to put feelings into words."

"I don't think—it's nothing to do with you, Edward. And not with me either."

"You know, the books you read, they say it's sex."

So he'd been reading books; she hadn't known. Maybe he read them at lunchtime, and kept them locked in his office desk.

"This one book by a New York psychiatrist, he says that if the sex adjustment is all right, everything else in the marriage will be fine."

"There's nothing wrong with sex," she said, "not for me."

"Not me either."

They were both silent for a moment, remembering. She felt the familiar flood of blood and heat—only a ghost now, faint and barely recognizable.

"It's something else," she said.

Because his eyes were glittering as bright as if there were Christmas tree lights behind them, she reached out and touched his cheek, bristly and blue-shadowed. He was sweating heavily, the stubble was slippery with moisture. He smelled sweaty too, heavy and musky.

They made love there on the couch, quick and uncomfortable. Then in bed, comfortable and insatiable. They both overslept and were late for work in the morning.

But the words remained. They hung in the living room air; they hung, muted, over the bed. The words had been heard, had danced through ears and rattled in heads: More than this?

Mary Margaret shook herself back to the present, turned off the TV. To say something, anything, she asked: "Pa, isn't that a new road sign out front? The curve sign?"

"No," her father said.

"Looks new to me."

"No," her father said. "They put that sign there three, four years ago."

"You ready for dinner?" her mother said.

That meant the casserole was already on the table.

"Wait a minute, Ma. I've got to tell you something, something important. Edward and I are going to get a divorce."

They stared at her blankly.

"It's not that there's anything wrong between us." (How could she explain when she was so uncertain herself?) "We just thought it would be better this way." (But maybe it wouldn't.) "Edward got a big promotion and a transfer to the Houston office. He'll leave in a couple of weeks, they want him right away. And I'm not going with him."

Not seeming to hear, her father walked out the front door, slowly, putting his feet down in the manner of very heavy men. He crossed the lawn to check the date stenciled on the sign, then came back to the house. "Seventy-eight." The climb had left him puffing slightly. "Like I said, 8-22-78, three years ago. Clear as can be."

The sound of the closing front door, muted by thick weather stripping, set echoes bouncing in Mary Margaret's head: *More than this. There must be more than this.*

"Did you listen, Pa? Did you hear what I said?"

"He's got to do one thing at a time," her mother said. "You asked him about the sign."

Always on his side, Mary Margaret thought. You're alike as twins.

"Edward and I are still friends, but we want a divorce and that's what we're going to get."

"Catholic people don't get divorced," her mother said.

Her father said, "The Slob walked out on you."

I have honored these people, she thought, I have honored them for all my twenty-nine years, and I am not about to stop now.

"His name is Edward, and he didn't leave me. We agreed to separate, both of us."

"You want to eat dinner?" her mother said to her father.

They heaved themselves out of their chairs and went to the table.

The words were still echoing. Hers? Or Edward's? *More than this.*

Her parents ate steadily, she only pushed the noodles across her plate, separating the bits of tuna, the peas.

"You don't want to eat?" her mother said. "You got to eat to keep your strength up."

"I'm not hungry."

Her father said, "You're not going to keep that apartment?"

"Just for a couple of weeks," she said.

"You got to think of where to live."

Mary Margaret pushed a red fleck of pimiento to the rim of her plate. "Yes."

Her mother folded her hands. With her heavy sloping shoulders and small head topped by a cone of black hair she was a perfect pyramid. "Her room's still here."

"How would it look," her father said. "Her living here, married and without a husband and divorced."

"How it looks?" her mother repeated hesitantly.

"Who'd care," Mary Margaret said. "Who'd know. Who ever comes here?"

Only their blood, their cousins, on special holidays and saint's days and Communion days, when white-dressed children went from house to house, bringing with them innocence and spiritual grace. And good luck. Her father said he always brought in his longest shots on Communion days.

Now they were telling her she wasn't welcome back. That her parents' house was closed. . . . Except for Wednesday supper and perpetual novena.

I must tell Edward that, she thought, as soon as I get home. He'll love that and we'll have a good laugh.

He'd be waiting for her—she was certain. Sex was now a hunger for them, demanding, painful, then satisfied and comfortable. They were so happy together, they were friends. In two weeks they would separate, with a kiss.

Maybe, she thought, that's all there is.

Her mother was saying with unusual emphasis, "She can come back here, Al. I want her to come back here." She wiped the perspiration from her fat cheeks with her paper napkin. "I don't care what you or anybody says."

Well, Mary Margaret thought wryly, scratch one, but the old mare came through. . . . And aloud she said, "I didn't know you thought so much about appearances, Pa."

"It's her room." Her mother was shivering—anger or nervousness—her pudgy shoulders shook and a sharp smell of old woman's sweat came from her.

"Wait, Ma," Mary Margaret said, "you didn't let me finish. I'm changing jobs too and I'm moving. To Oklahoma City."

Slowly her father got up and took the paperbound *Texaco Atlas of the United States* from the corner bookshelf. (They'd gotten it years before, when they drove to Florida. It was their first and only vacation, they hated every minute.) He unfolded the largest map and put it on the table.

Mary Margaret pointed. "There. Right there."

Everything had happened at once. The evening they decided on divorce, the very same evening Edward told her he'd be moving to Houston, they went out to dinner. It was an Italian restaurant—checkered tablecloths and candles in wine bottles and the heavy greasy pasta they both liked. They finished a bottle of wine and became giggly and secretive, heads together, holding hands and touching knees.

We must look like lovers, she thought, and we are. In a way.

"Look." Edward was playing with her hand, twirling the silver and amethyst ring he'd given her for Christmas. "Are you really going to stay here? Won't it be a little rough for you, I mean?"

"I've got my parents," she said.

They both smiled warmly at the joke.

He insisted: "My boss, you know him, Hank Cavendish, he's being transferred, it's a big step up for him. He wanted his secretary to go with him, but she won't leave. I bet anything he'd jump at the chance to hire you if you'd relocate right away."

"Why not?" she said, giggling, the wine still singing in her ears. "Why not. Where?"

"Oklahoma City."

"Where's that?"

"I don't know," he said. "I do know it'll be a good move for you. They're expecting that office to grow pretty fast. Wherever it is."

She told her parents: "I get a twenty per cent raise, plus medical and dental coverage, plus they are paying my moving expenses."

They nodded. Figures were something they had no difficulty understanding.

"Will you be coming next Wednesday?" her mother said.

"Next Wednesday. But not the one after that."

Her mother nodded, the twisted knot of gray and black hair moved up and down slowly.

Don't you want to ask when I will be back? If I will come back? If I'll be here at Christmas? If I'll come back for your funerals? Do you never worry about anything?

"Time to go." Her father pushed himself up from the table. The atlas lay open, one page soaking in the vinegar of his salad plate.

Go? Where would they go, who never went anywhere? The novena. The Wednesday perpetual novena.

Her mother smoothed back her hair in the sideboard mirror, her father went to put on his leather shoes.

If I stay any longer, I am going to break every dish on the table, or I am going to throw a chair through that window, or I am going to scream and keep on screaming. I am going to dishonor my father and my mother. If I don't get out of here.

Her chair, pushed too hard, slid back into the wall. The

picture of her mother's first husband shivered and slipped sidewise.

"I'm not going," she said. Then louder, for her father who was still in the bedroom: "I'm not going to the novena."

"You always go," her mother said.

Her father came to the doorway, one shoe still in his hand.

Four eyes, surprised, accusing, puzzled, shocked.

Don't look at me. You are my parents but don't look at me that way. You've had all you can have from me. One novena more is too much.

"I'll go next week," she said. "For the last time, next week."

They both nodded to her, pyramids of flesh with tiny heads perched on top, like kindergarten drawings.

She hurried through the living room, snatching her coat and purse as she went. Running with fear from something she didn't know, something that might not have been there, something that might even have loved her.

She drove off, tires squealing, leaving the thing that had chased her growling emptily at the end of the driveway.

By the time she got to the crowded highway, she felt better, the soft singing of the engine comforted her. She opened the window and familiar exhaust-laden air curled across her face and shoulders.

It was a very warm night, she thought. As her mother had said, she hadn't really needed to bring her coat.

WIDOW'S
WALK

Myra Rowland stopped her bright red jeep at the entrance to the beach club. Over the iron gates decorative bunting hung dusty and limp, shivering uncertainly in the small currents of midday air. It was the first day of the new summer season.

"Morning, Frank," she called to the uniformed guard. "It's nice to see you back again."

"Hot morning, Mrs. Rowland." He pushed open the gate. "Is that a new jeep?"

"I liked the color."

"It sure is bright." He leaned against the car door and nodded to the empty seat beside her. "Mr. Rowland didn't come with you?"

"We lost him," she said softly. "This winter. In January."

He hesitated, slow to understand. Then he pulled his hand away as if the door were burning hot. "I didn't know that. I'm sorry."

She said, "One learns to live with it. Like any other fact."

She drove through the gates, thinking: Why did I say anything so silly? Why did I say I had lost Hugh? I haven't lost him at all. I know exactly where he is and the headstone says HUGH DUDLEY ROWLAND 1905–1984.

The neat narrow blacktopped road stretched ahead of her; she drove precisely down the very middle. Thinking: Hugh and I came here every good sunny day for thirty summers. We were one of the families who bought this land, built the first clubhouse. Not more than a shed in the jack pines. When the 1961 hurricane destroyed it, Hugh said: Good riddance. This time I'll lend the club money for a proper building.

That building still stood (its loan long repaid), quite small and lost in all the subsequent remodelings and expansions. But there. It was Hugh who had gone.

She had never felt the presence of his ghost, never seen faint images or slight motions in the air. She never felt that he lingered behind, fading slightly perhaps, following her into this summer.

A decisive man, he had left her completely. A quiet man, he had slipped away quietly.

After the funeral, surfeited with kisses and tears, staggering under the burden of organ chords, she'd returned to their house alone. She'd insisted on that. Not the housekeeper, not her son, not the dogs. She closed the door firmly behind her. The metallic click of the latch fell like a marble and rolled through the silent empty rooms. After a pause, leaning against the door, drawing strength from the firm unmoving wood, she climbed the stairs. Deliberately, being careful of her balance, of her breathing, a high-wire walker moving between two points. In the bedroom she sat, spine stretched alertly, hands on knees, palms up, like boats stranded by the tide. As she waited, her eyes moved slowly, meticulously covering every inch of the room. Up and down the walls, applying her surveillance like a methodical painter, slipping beneath the pictures, passing across the surfaces of the furniture. Across the floor, like a careful housekeeper, board by board, diving under rugs to survey them from beneath. And finally reaching the bed, where Hugh had died three days past, where her eyes now traced every flower on its quilted neutral emptiness.

Later, sometime during the night, she stood up, cramped and chill, and walked through the house. She went into every single room, looked into every closet, opening and closing curtains, turning lamps on and off and on again, then returning to change the pattern of light and shadow she had just made. Picking up vases and boxes and ashtrays and figures and paperweights, taking books from their shelves, turning them over once, twice, putting them back. Pressing her palms on the polished surfaces of tables and desks and chairs, then wiping away the sweaty imprints with her scarf or the edge of her skirt. Repeating, over and over.

When the late winter sun rose, yellow and thin, she was dazzled by the radiance, bending her head before its glory, hands over eyes.

In the blazing white sun of July, Myra Rowland drove her jeep along the twin strips of black asphalt that led to the beach. The road was a large semicircle through wind-shaped olives and rhododendrons (with a few late flowers in the deep cool places), through small salt-twisted pin oaks, through leathery rugosa roses covered with flat pink and white flowers. The stretches of shiny-leaved poison ivy were beginning to show blotches of yellow—the gardeners had been spraying weed killer. Nearest the shore, roots firmly planted in the dry thin ground, jack pines crowded the road, the shadows of their grove the blackish green of the ocean bottom.

The road lifted over a low hill. The red jeep popped, like a cork from a bottle, into the glare of the beach.

The ocean, blue in its distance and deep green inshore, was rumpled and creased by wind squalls. A fleet of small boats raced toward a distant orange marker, tacking back and forth, white sails bisecting the ruffled shadows. The beach itself was smooth and curved, backed by tall dunes spotted with tall sparse grasses. At the center was the clubhouse, gleaming with fresh white paint and newly washed windows, American flag and club ensign flying over the roof. On each side of the building, like outstretched wings, were dozens of brilliantly colored beach umbrellas. The breeze, onshore this time of day, was heavy with the sound of people: the hum of voices and the cries of children, high and thin like the calls of distant seabirds.

I do not want to go there, Myra thought, I do not want to go into that jumble of sound and color. I don't want to enter the giant bubble of their breathing, these summer friends whom I have not seen for ten months.

Then she felt, as she sometimes did, a pressure in the small of her back, pushing her forward. And she heard a laugh—a cackle of profound derision—deep inside her skull.

She shifted the jeep into four-wheel drive, swung hard to the right, and accelerated directly across the dunes, dodging between signs that forbade such passage as ecologically damaging, bouncing at last into the parking lot, into the space neatly marked MRS. ROWLAND, SR. (Hugh's name had vanished even from there, she thought, even that small piece of wood had been corrected to reflect the new fact.)

She climbed out slowly, massaging an arthritic ache in her left hip. There was a tangle of wild beach pea vine caught in the car bumper—she snapped off four small pink flowers and tucked them into the band of her large pink beach hat. She picked up a canvas bag filled with sun lotions and walked briskly down the sloping flower-lined path to the club.

Harry Marshall was sitting at his favorite table, the one in the far corner of the deck, the one with the best view of the entrance. He'd come early, as he always did, and settled down in the greenish reflected shade of the overhead umbrella. He liked to be the first to greet his friends on the opening day of the summer season.

"Well now," he said. "Myra's here."

"Who?" Bill Landrieux, his brother-in-law and law partner in the days before they both retired, was admiring his tequila sunrise, turning it around slowly. "They weren't this color last summer," he said. "They taste the same but they aren't the same color."

"Myra's here," Harry Marshall repeated.

Slowly, reluctantly, Bill Landrieux put down his glass. "Myra Rowland?"

"She just arrived."

Bill peered vaguely toward the path through the dunes. "Is that her in the bright pink dress?"

"Contacts not working, Bill?"

"You know I can't wear contacts with the damn sand."

"Get prescription sunglasses, you vain old goat."

"These are prescription. I got to get a new doctor." He pulled off the glasses and squinted into the glare. "I see better without the damn things. Sure, that's Myra Rowland. Always wears pink. Hugh isn't with her."

"Hugh died last winter. I clipped the obituary and sent it to you."

"You did? I guess Jane forgot to give it to me. You know, Harry, I think that woman must have Alzheimer's. She can't remember anything."

"Jane always was that way." Harry waved to Myra Rowland, who had stopped to admire the flowering begonias.

Bill popped back his sunglasses. "The glare gives me a headache without them."

The combination of heat and alcohol was getting to him, Harry thought. Sweat gleamed through his thin blond hair. "Maybe you should go a little slower on the drinks, Bill. Can't have you passing out."

Bill ignored him and continued staring at Myra, who had finished with the flowers. "So old Hugh's dead. What'd he die of?"

"The paper didn't say."

"Old age, I guess. What was he? Eighty?"

"Seventy-nine."

"I sure hope Jane wrote her a note, but she probably forgot that too."

Harry stood up, waving and calling, "Myra, good to see you. Come sit with us for a bit."

Myra smiled politely and warmly while she struggled to remember their names. It was so long from summer to summer, she thought. Hugh had been good at names. Hugh had always remembered for her.

"How nice to see you again." A name popped into her memory: Harry Marshall. That was right. And Bill something or other. "You both look wonderful," she said, brightening up her smile. "Just wonderful."

"We're still at the same old table." Bill laughed. "And that's probably the same old umbrella up there."

"Same table, same umbrella, same drinks," Harry said. "Yours was a gin and tonic, right?"

"You have a fantastic memory." She sat down carefully in the canvas deck chair. Her back was very stiff today.

"I'll get the drinks," Harry said.

"One for me, brother-in-law," Bill called after him.

He was pretty drunk already, Myra noticed, his skin flushed so deeply that blood seemed ready to ooze from each pore. "And how is your wife?" she inquired politely.

"Jane's fine. She's down there on the beach with the grandchildren. But you knew about Edna?"

"Last summer seems such a long time ago."

"I know you remember Edna. Great friend of Jane's. Like a sister really, not just a summer friend. They used to have lunch together every Tuesday all winter long. Well, she died."

"Oh yes, of course," Myra said, "I do remember her." A short thin wiry woman who played a fine game of tennis. Myra had disliked her, her nervousness and constant movement.

"Cancer," Bill said, wiping the sweat from his bald head. "Everywhere, even her brain. Doctors couldn't do anything. They didn't even try."

All that flitting vibration stopped, Myra thought wearily, all those jerking muscles and racing feet.

Harry Marshall put the tray of drinks down on the table. "Here's to the summer!"

Bill lifted his glass. "To us old folks. We made another year." Then blushing, remembering, "I didn't really mean that the way it sounded, Myra. I'm awfully sorry about Hugh. I really am. He was one great guy."

"I don't talk about it any more." Myra saw relief smooth out the squinched agitation on his face.

"We bought a place in the Bahamas," Harry said, changing the subject. "A little pink cottage with bougainvillea on the fence. The house is all right, but it was that bougainvillea that sold me. It's pink like you wouldn't believe."

Bill said, "And right away Jane's got to go see her dear brother's house. And once she sees it, she wants one too. So we're looking. The funniest thing, Myra, would you believe they've got a beach club that looks almost exactly like this one."

"Except for the pine trees," Harry added. "No pine trees."

"So you have an eternal summer," Myra said. "How nice, how very nice."

Harry beamed. "What a wonderful way to look at it, Myra. I suppose that's exactly what it is. We're retired and living in an eternal summer. Damn poetic, that's what it is."

Liam Thorpe, who was stretched full length on one of the blue padded lounges, lifted his head and squinted across the deck. "Isabel, isn't that Myra Rowland?"

His wife, who was lying face down, said, "I heard she came early this year, a couple of weeks ago."

"Did you remember to write her after Hugh died?"

"I always remember."

"She came alone this year?"

"In a manner of speaking."

"Now what the hell's that supposed to mean."

"Her two grandsons came with her. And she's still got that housekeeping couple she's had all these years. And her son and his wife will be down every weekend."

"You are a veritable treasure trove of information."

"I met her son in the post office." Isabel chuckled smugly. "He also told me that they've booked in a steady series of guests. So that's why I said that in a way she wasn't alone."

"Well, she sure has room for everybody in that big old house." Liam lay back, talking to the heat-hazed sky. "Hugh Rowland's dead. And ... Isabel, hasn't there been an awful lot of that this winter? I mean, an unusual amount of dying."

"I don't think so." Isabel's voice was muffled by the folded towel over her head. "Of course at our age you do have to expect a certain amount, I guess."

"But so many? I mean, that's not natural. There was Hugh, and there was that awful woman Edna. And Sally and Andrew, remember them?"

"Liam, they were killed in a plane crash. That's not the same at all."

"They aren't here, that's all I'm counting."

Isabel's legs began to move restlessly. "Don't be silly."

"And then there was Webster. Ed Webster."

"He'd have been close to ninety."

"We're not that far away, duck."

Her head jerked up, the towel slid to her shoulders. "Liam, you are nowhere near ninety and neither am I. Don't exaggerate."

"And Roger. Remember him, Roger Fasterling?"

Isabel began turning over, slowly sighing with annoyance.

"How many is that?" he asked the sky. "It's a lot."

Isabel completed her roll and settled down on her back. Eyes closed, she began rubbing sun lotion on her face. "Well, Liam, however many people died, there are still plenty left. The place is positively packed. Just look down the beach."

"Kids," he said.

"And up here," she insisted. "This deck is as crowded as I've ever seen it."

"Another thing." Liam sat up. "I don't know half the people here. I remember how it used to be. It used to be I could walk up and down and know every face I passed. I could sit down and talk to just anybody and everybody."

"You can still do that."

"What would I say? What do you want me to say? Who are you? Or maybe: I knew your grandfather when he was alive."

"You could say: I like to meet people I don't know."

"I'd just look senile."

"Oh, for God's sake!" Isabel bounced up and down irritably, the padded cushions squeaking. "This whole thing is utterly silly. Next year I am going to wait until everybody has finished counting and knows who died over the winter and who's too sick to be here." She swiped her towel at a passing deerfly. "On opening day this whole place sounds like a bunch of lunatic gardeners: Did it survive the winter? Did it survive in good shape? Has it had a little stroke, nothing serious? . . . God, what crazy accounting."

"But you haven't said we're wrong," Liam insisted. "Only that you don't want to hear us."

Isabel put the folded towel across her face, carefully, deliberately, then lifted one corner to say, "Tell me if Myra comes this way."

Myra Rowland changed into her bathing suit, moving and bending with careful deliberation. The locker room maid, she noticed, was the same as last year: a college girl, short, bespectacled, silent.

"Hello," Myra said.

The young woman looked up from her book, flashing brilliant blue eyes at the bottom of deep lens pools. And smiled faintly.

"Studying?" Myra asked politely as she gathered her beach towel and hat.

The blue eyes blinked, vanishing behind their lids. Stubby fingers held up a book. Myra glanced at it: something about the endocrine system.

Good lord, she sits in this damp locker room and studies that. A silent blue-eyed toad under a rock.

"See you later," Myra said.

The head nodded slightly, tipped, it seemed, by the weight of its glasses.

The sand was very hot to her feet and she hurried to the water, tossing her things on a vacant lounge.

I need bathing shoes, she thought. I did have a pair once, years ago. But Hugh disliked them. Those things make you look like a grandmotherly washerwoman, he said. . . . I wonder if I still have them at the house, put away in a box somewhere.

She stood in the cool sand at the very edge of the water, curling her toes in the damp softness.

At once her two grandsons appeared, swimming rapidly to stand next to her. Gleaming sleek creatures, smooth muscles under taut skin.

She smiled at them, noticing for the uncounted thousandth time how very much they resembled Hugh.

For a second or so she allowed herself the comforting thought that they were Hugh, that he was here, in them, young and strong and healthy, younger even than when she'd first met him. . . . The idea flitted, soothed, vanished with a tiny pop like a bubble.

Hugh did not live in them. Hugh was dead. She was here alone.

Oh, but they were good boys, they were wonderful boys. So well-mannered that they truly seemed to enjoy keeping Grandmother company. . . . And she was glad to have them. Glad to warm herself at the glow of their youth and health.

"This first day, today, is very hard for me," she told them, explaining calmly and carefully. "Last year I was here with your grandfather. This year it's very difficult for me to come to the same place without him."

Two pairs of brown eyes watched her, understanding, patient, loving, obedient. Like fine spaniels.

"But none of that has anything to do with you. Go back to your friends," she said. "I'll have a swim and a bite of lunch and I'll go home early. I don't want to get too much sun the first day."

They were gone into the ocean then, like porpoises, arcing and playing, ribbons of wake behind.

The water was very cold, and she went in backwards, sinking down slowly in a kind of curtsy at the last. She swam out forty strokes, counting carefully, then sidestroked in. Her arthritis—stunned, she liked to think, by the combination of cold water and sudden exercise—did not twinge or ache as she walked back across the sand to the deck. She toweled her hair quickly and stretched out on her lounge, face down, letting the sun dry her bathing suit. She could feel the rays, like a dentist's drill, vibrate against her spine.

Jane Landrieux and her daughter Linda sat on a large red and blue beach blanket littered with plastic toys—shovels and pails and sand sieves—and watched two lifeguards give swimming lessons to a line of small children.

"Mother," Linda said, "do you think they learn anything like that? I mean, those lessons aren't cheap."

Jane's eyes found her granddaughter in the shrieking crowd. "Well, I think she's learning. She just hasn't got the breathing right, that's all."

"That's *all!* That's the important part, Mother."

"I love her haircut. It makes her look, well, French."

"I'm not sure I like it."

"Watch out! Deerfly." Jane swatted at her leg. "Got him, bury him quick."

"Mother, you've got to kill them or they'll dig right up out of the sand."

Jane said, looking off across the beach, over the crowded heads and through the forest of umbrellas, "Isn't that Myra Rowland?"

"Pink bathing suit? Yes. I saw her earlier, sitting at Papa's table."

"Her husband died last winter."

"You sent us a newspaper clipping, remember?"

"I meant to," Jane said. "I just didn't think I had."

"I wonder why she came back."

"It's a beautiful house with a lovely view. She must like it."

"But she's got enough money to go anywhere." Linda was again watching the children thrashing about in the shallows.

"She must like it here."

"Can't," Linda said firmly. "No way."

"Then I don't know." Jane reached for her paperback to end the conversation.

Myra Rowland, bones warmed and joints comforted by the sun, gathered her towel and bag and hat, and prepared to go home. Her eyes, dazzled by the glare, wrapped the contours of the world—the beach, the buildings, the people— in a gleaming radiance. She floated through a blurred and glorious landscape, in a halo of light, through shimmering featureless ephemera.

She stopped at the bar for a gin and tonic, her second of the day, her last at the club. After this she would change and go home to sit in the green coolness of her garden, next to the heavy arcing canes of the Mermaid rosebush she herself had planted forty years before. She would have another gin and tonic and then another, less mixer each time, until finally she drank straight gin on the rocks. At eight her grandsons, houseguests, and visitors would have dinner in the dining room. Usually she joined them, though the food tasted of nothing and the wine was harsh as vinegar and she grew bored and fretful at the sound of voices. Some evenings, increasingly many evenings now, she did not go in to dinner. When she left the garden she moved, slowly and steadily, ship under full sail, through the hall—passing the dining room door without a nod, without a glance—to the stairs. She lifted and pointed her chin, following it like a compass needle. Up the wide polished stairs to the second floor where the bedrooms were, then other steps to the third floor, with its servants' rooms and storage closets. Coming at last to a steep and narrow climb, hardly more than an enclosed ladder, where she balanced herself with palms pressed against the walls on each side. Up through the roof to the very top. The widow's walk.

It was a small platform, four steps each way, edged by a low wooden railing and benches with blue canvas cushions. (Crisp and bright this beginning of summer, they'd be blotched with mildew by September.)

She paced the four-step pattern, back and forth. (They could hear her footfalls on the floor immediately below.) She watched the constellations swing up out of the ocean and traced the twin bands of the Milky Way. Mosquitoes buzzed softly about her ears, and owls in their passing tore silent holes in the night. Occasionally from below there'd be human sounds, filtered by distance: mumbled voices, laughter like a match flaring, a piano badly played.

Eventually, she would stretch out on the blue canvas cushions and stare at the sky overhead, listening to the songs the planets sang and the rattle of shingle on the beach in a falling tide. Usually she'd fall asleep, sound, dreamless sleep, waking only to first light and bird cries, her hair drenched and dripping with dew and night fog, her lips smiling with a quiet joy.

In the sun of midafternoon Myra Rowland picked up her gin and tonic from the bar and looked for an empty table.

"Myra! Here. Join us."

Her sun-diluted brain fumbled for a name and found it:

Isabel. Isabel something or other. And he was, what—an Irish name, yes. Liam. Of course.

She joined them, greeting them with the names she had so recently retrieved from her memory. And then they seemed to fade away from her, to dwindle, to diminish. She lost all interest in them. She fell silent, nodding now and then, drinking steadily, sleepy, eyes half-closed.

"Look, Myra, are you sure you're all right?"

She heard them distinctly but faintly. She opened her eyes, lifted her chin. And smiled. Their figures grew, fleshed out, they were human again. "I am perfectly all right," she said. "You must just be patient with an old woman."

Overhead a navy blue umbrella, faded and streaked by last season's sun, trapped shimmering swirls of hot air under its dome. They were, the three of them, stained by its reflected light, the color of new bruises.

"I am so happy to see you." She lifted her glass. Smiling with a delight that was real, very real, but had nothing to do with them. (They would be less pleased, she thought, were they to know that.) "To our summer," she said to their hazy haloed faces, "to our summer here."

Oh yes, my friends whose last name I cannot remember, I am truly glad to see you. I appreciate your kindness and your friendliness.

I am truly glad to have had this day, one of my dwindling supply, to have had the sun and the bitter sea taste in my mouth. I am glad to have my favorite drink and to hear its ice cubes rattle.

She lifted her glass again, higher, so that the umbrella's bluish stain poured through it.

And this sun-spoiled, sun-streaked ragged umbrella over my head—how beautiful it is to me there, where soon enough there'll be only earth.

Until then, though, the days, how they shine, how they shine.

HOUSEKEEPER

Yes, I was housekeeper there, five days a week, for nearly nine years. And there was grief and sadness at the beginning as well as the end, I'll tell you that.

I started work a month or so after my husband died. I didn't really need the money: I had his pension and the income from two rental properties we'd managed to buy over the years. But I just couldn't sit home and be grieved by ghosts and wet the floor with tears.

When they heard, my children got very upset. All of them—Alec and Marty and Crissie—who never agreed on anything in their lives, they all agreed that I mustn't work. No, Mama, they said by phone, by letter. No, no, please no. Alec, my oldest, even came to see me, came all the way across the country to tell me it wasn't decent for me to do housework.

"If there's anything you want, Mama, just tell us. We're all doing very well, we can give you anything you want."

I started to say: Give me your father back, healthy and laughing.

But I couldn't say that, not to those brown eyes glistening with confusion and worry. So, because he was my child and

I had had years of being patient with him, I tried to explain politely and carefully.

"I understand, Mama," he said. "We all understand that you want to be busy, to do something, to get out. Do you know that Mr. Congreve is looking for somebody to help in his office?"

So Alec had been talking to the minister, not telling me anything about it. That was typical Alec, he just had to organize things. But not this time.

You see, I figured I'd done my bit for the church over the years. I didn't think I owed it anything. And I didn't intend to spend my days typing notices and mailing out newsletters with all those other widows. Relicts, my grandmother used to call them.

Alec, I told him, you are a nice boy and a good son, but this is none of your business. I have done housework all my life, only this time it's going to be for pay and not for family.

So that was that, though he never gave up trying to get me to change my mind. And he told everybody that working was just a passing fancy of mine, that it wouldn't last.

Well, it did last, like I said, for nearly nine years. My first job was my last and only one. And that was because I found Dr. Hollisher.

He lived in one of the cottages on the beach at Indian Head Bay, a nice little house with wide screen porches all around and oak trees towering overhead, reaching right across the roof. It was so shady and cool in summer, he hardly ever used air-conditioning. Of course it was chilly and damp during the winter rains, but they don't last long.

His name was Milton Eugene Hollisher, so it said on the National City Bank checks he had ready for me every week, waiting on the hall table, same place every time, one end tucked under the big brass hurricane lamp. He never once gave me my check directly, hand to hand.

He told me he was retired. I heard somewhere, at church maybe or at the grocery, that he'd been a psychiatrist at the big VA hospital at Greenwood, but I don't know for sure. He didn't talk about himself.

We got on just fine. He was one for putting things plainly and I always did like to have everything clearly understood.

"Mrs. Emmons," he said to me the very first time I went there—almost but not quite inside the front door, he was waiting for me on the porch—"you are on time to the minute, I admire that." He waved me to a cane rocking chair. (It was one of those screen porches with rockers and plant stands full of ferns and a ceiling fan turning slowly.) "I should like you to come at ten and leave at two or earlier, if possible. Please do not play the radio. The only television in the house is a single black and white set which is tuned to my evening news station. It is so very small it can hardly tempt you to turn it on. Please do not whistle or sing at your work. That was splendid for Snow White, but I do not think it is suitable for this house."

I sat in his rocker. And looked around. The porch was spotless, not even a speck of dust on the shiny glass table-top, though it was a dry summer and fine blowing haze hung all day in the air. He must have wiped it clean just before I came.

And I, to use his words, admire that. To have things neat for the housekeeper to start off—yes, I did like that.

There was a large nest of mud daubers building in the outside corner of the porch. I pointed to it. "You should do something about that. They'll be inside pretty soon, you know."

"I am very allergic to stings," he said, scarcely looking at it.

"I'll take care of it with a spray can."

He nodded.

I realized then that we were talking as if I had the job already. As if he'd asked me, which he hadn't, and I'd accepted, which I hadn't either.

"And of course," he said, "you will have to wear other shoes."

I looked at my feet: black oxfords, the most comfortable shoes in the world.

"They have crepe soles," he said. "I do not like people to walk silently."

"Well," I said slowly, "most people prefer the quiet."

He shook his head violently.

"All right," I said.

I tried for a week. My bunions burned and my spine ached, and I went back to my rubber-soled shoes. He was upset all right. I had to tell him I couldn't work otherwise—anyway, he gave up about the shoes. Eventually I thought of a solution. Years ago, when I was a girl, we all wore charm bracelets with dozens of odd shapes dangling and rattling. I hunted up my bracelet—took me a while to find it—and wore it to work every day. I felt like one of those fat pet cats who wear silver bells to warn away birds. But it satisfied him.

Months later, out of the blue, he said, "You know, I've grown to like the sound of your bracelet."

"I'm reliving my youth," I said. "This thimble, see, that's my tenth birthday, and the bell was my fourteenth. My husband brought me that Eiffel Tower from Paris when he came back after the war."

By that time, Dr. Hollisher had walked away. He could never manage to listen or say more than a dozen words before hurrying off with a busy distracted air. Like a man who has more to do than he will ever manage. In truth, of course, he had nothing to do but amuse himself and all day to do it in.

Still the sound of the silver was bright and cheery. And the memories kept me from being bored. After a while, though I was doing the work (I suppose I was doing it properly; he never complained), I wasn't there at all, not in the house on Indian Head Bay. I was years away. I even found I liked thinking about the past. I'd never done that before. All my attention had been needed in each and every day, first with the children and then Ed, my husband, and his illness. In a way the past was like that bracelet, locked up in a drawer, unnoticed and unthought about.

So, one by one, I remembered all the times suspended there in silver links. Birthdays and parties when I was young. A peach chiffon dress, ankle-length with a ruffle at the hem. Rooms that were filled with giggles and the funny smells of children, a little like wet puppies, a little like fresh bread.

That bracelet kept me company as I polished and dusted and sprayed Windex and swept the leaves from the steps.

"You are smiling," Dr. Hollisher said to me once. "Why?"

But of course he didn't wait for my answer. Soon I heard the screen door close with a little soft hiss—he had automatic closing mechanisms on all the doors, he hated them to slam—then his car start. And I went back to putting paste wax on the metal porch furniture. In this climate it's the only way to stop rust.

Wearing that bracelet, I went from child to young woman. The wonder days, that's what they were. When everything had a high Technicolor light, all girls were beautiful, all boys were handsome. When danger and uncertainty varnished everything, even the simplest, with excitement and importance and pain and joy. When young men went to war, leaving their pictures on pianos and mantelpieces, linked to home by a thin chain of V-mail letters and food packages and sometimes War Department telegrams.

Nothing lasts, not even remembered glory—after a while I wore out my memories. Like a plate put in the dishwasher too often, they just faded. The gold edges flaked off first, then the shine and the pattern, and then it was just a used-up bit of nothing.

When that happened, I stopped wearing the bracelet. I packed it in the box with my high school yearbook, my bronze medal in Seventh Grade Statewide Spelling, my plaque as District Homemaker of the Ninth Grade, and a couple of pressed gardenias. Then I put the whole thing back where it had been, the top shelf of the hall closet, next to the old photograph albums.

If Dr. Hollisher missed my jingling bracelet, he didn't say anything. Myself, I don't think he really noticed. By then, you see, he was used to me and he didn't have to think about me at all. He could go about his own business, do what he was interested in doing. And he was interested in so many things.

Like radio. For a couple of years he took courses in electronics at the community college in Buena Vista. (My cousin, who was a secretary there, saw him: bald head in a room full of kids just out of high school.) One day a steel tower went up next to the house, and a lot of expensive radio equipment went in the small back bedroom. (He called the Salvation Army to take away the furniture that had been in there.) He had endless trouble with the antenna, that tall tripod with its flopping crossbars, like a high-wire acrobat's poles. The upper section was supposed to move up and down, to improve reception at certain times, but the electric motor never really worked. Servicemen came time after time to tinker with it, some gray-suited engineers stood around and stared at it. One of them told me the antenna would never work properly and Dr. Hollisher should scrap it and begin all over again. I didn't think that was very likely, but I left a note repeating the message anyway.

Even if it wasn't perfect, the antenna did work. Neighbors told me lights burned in that room all hours of the night. He began keeping careful radio logbooks, lining them up on the new shelves he'd bought. He even went back to school to learn Portuguese, to understand better some of the people he could now talk to.

Then too he had his chess. He was a very enthusiastic player. He'd turned the second extra bedroom (the house had three) into a study, with a couch and a big soft armchair. He played chess there.

He had games going on all over the world, people he never even saw. The best was a man in Spokane, but there was also a Catholic priest in Belgium, a car dealer in Mexico City, somebody in Chicago who used official government business envelopes; there was a book publisher in London and a retired colonel in Hawaii who signed with just his initials: VSC. Dr. Hollisher recorded each game in its own ledger. He was very methodical.

And for each game he had a different board. Really different—there was a cheap plastic one, and a very expensive one in cast pewter, a rough carved wooden one (a patient gave me that, he said), a modern one of black and white stone. The strangest was a very large one with ivory pieces four inches high, and all the figures naked. King and knight had the bodies of athletes; bishop was old and thin with fasting; queen was beautiful and seductive; pawn was a crouched fat dwarf.

Dr. Hollisher kept all the boards in a row. How do you

remember which is which? I asked him. Why, he said, each player's set suits him perfectly. I recognize them at once.

Who was the naked board? I wondered, but I couldn't seem to ask.

He played a lot of cards too. Wednesday was always poker night at his house. He'd ask me to make sandwiches—ham and roast beef, no tuna salad, and no lettuce, ever—and he'd fill the refrigerator with beer.

Tuesday was his bridge group. About every six weeks it would be his turn, and I would set up the tables and arrange things properly. He had a caterer bring in the little sandwiches and the salads and the fancy petits fours. He'd buy extra ice and check his whiskey supply and put half a dozen bottles of white wine in the refrigerator. And in the morning I'd find crumbs and sprinkles of sugar all over the living and dining rooms, and long lines of black ants marching up out of the garden to carry them away.

I suppose he had other friends, like any retired man would, but they never called during the morning when I was there. If the phone rang, it was always the contractor or the plumber or Belters Electronics with some new theory about why his antenna didn't work. Once it was the community college registrar to say that they'd lost his forms, would he stop by the office, please. And occasionally, it was a woman named Judy.

"She's called twice already today," I said to him when he walked in.

"I know." He put the message slip in his pocket.

He didn't return the call, not while I was there.

Usually she spoke brusquely and quickly, like I was some

sort of answering device. But once she said, "He can't make up his mind, can he? And he never could."

"Is that a message?" I asked, quiet and polite.

"Yes." And she slapped down the phone.

To him I said, "Judy called again, the message is on the pad."

He said, "Thank you."

"Who is Judy?"

"My daughter." And he went out into the garden to tend his camellias. He was beginning to be interested in the problems of hybridizing, enough to enroll in a course at the state university, even though that meant a hundred-mile drive each week. Distances didn't seem to mean anything to him. The people at the gas station told me that he was there three or four times a week, filling up. He kept busy all right, but he didn't seem frantic or restless, at least not to me. He even slept very peacefully: his bed was barely mussed in the mornings, the covers still smooth and tight. He must have slipped inside very carefully, like a letter into an envelope.

Of course he did have very precise ideas. Once he had the painters completely redo the living room and dining room because they hadn't used the exactly right shade of pale blue. He wasn't being mean or stubborn; he just knew exactly what he wanted and he had to have it. Things were very important to him.

Prissy old maid—that's what his neighbors thought. I got to know them all. You can't come day after day and not have a talking friendship with the people on the other side of the fences. (With him it was a nod and a smile and how are you without stopping.) And they were all so curious about him—as if an old man living alone was somehow remarkable and strange. Only once did something unusual happen.

One evening, at suppertime, they told me, a blue Buick with rental plates parked in the drive and a woman with dark hair and a yellow dress went in the house. A long noisy argument began, very long and very noisy.

Dr. Hollisher closed all the windows and drew the curtains but indistinct mumbling voices still drifted on the damp night air. Around midnight—the neighbors all stayed up long past their usual bedtimes—the woman walked into the back garden and shouted, "What are you doing with all these fucking flowers?" (Mrs. Herbert, the right side neighbor, blushed when she told me.) For a few minutes the woman walked up and down in the garden, grabbing at plants and trying to pull them out. She managed to uproot a few day lilies and a row of daisies, but the bigger azalea and camellia bushes gave her only handfuls of leaves and small twigs. Blazing angry, she put her foot against a camellia trunk and kicked, losing her balance to fall full length in the soft greasy soil. Dr. Hollisher, who'd been standing silently in a corner of the porch, helped her up and back inside.

After that, things grew quiet, though the lights stayed on until daylight. The neighbors were beginning to think about calling the sheriff when the dark-haired woman appeared again, jumped in her car, and drove away, leaving twin streaks of rubber on the concrete. Dr. Hollisher watched her go.

Of course when I came some hours later, I had to hear all about it. Every one of the neighbors rushed to my car and told me the story through the windows. By the time I entered the house, I figured I'd heard everything and it wasn't any of my business. I was intending to go about my work as if nothing at all had happened.

Dr. Hollisher was waiting for me in the kitchen, drinking coffee. That in itself was pretty surprising: usually he only drank tea. Otherwise he seemed no different, he was shaved and dressed neatly as always. He did not even seem sleepy. "You will find a great deal of disorder in the house," he told me quietly. "Most unfortunate. A quantity of garden soil has been tracked in and there are cigarette ashes just about everywhere. I myself noticed at least four butts go into the blue cloisonné vase on the desk. My daughter arrived last evening and chose to make a public scene. She is my only child. Her mother and I divorced years ago and she subsequently died. Please tell that to the neighbors, who will be curious."

Actually the house wasn't half as bad as he seemed to think. It only took some work to get it back in order, some extra sweeping and vacuuming. The door to the room with his broadcasting equipment had been locked, so nothing was out of place there. The second bedroom was a mess. His daughter had slept there—the bed was rumpled, the sheets and pillows tossed about. There was a spilled ashtray and a large burn hole in the rug, a broken glass in the corner and a smashed plate. All the chessboards were upset—thrown across the room, it seemed.

I stayed a bit later that day to get it picked up and cleaned. The odor of cigarettes and spilled whiskey hung in the air for a day or so, but that was all. When the rugs came back from the cleaners, Dr. Hollisher set up his chessboards again, checked his ledgers and returned the pieces to their proper positions.

He was a very patient man.

Eventually Dr. Hollisher got interested in boats. Which wasn't surprising—his house was right on Indian Head Bay, his lawn sloped down to the sand. First he built a pier. Many people had them—a twenty-, thirty-foot catwalk to a small rickety platform. The sort of thing you wouldn't mind losing to the fall hurricanes. Years ago, when I was young, the town had its own pier—a huge platform a hundred feet out over the water, palm-roofed. All day long there'd be fishermen there, and crabbers. At night, the warm nights, young people would come from up and down the coast. You could hear them laughing and singing half a mile away. And it was lovely there, with the tiny colored lights shining along the roof and the moon showing streaks on the water, mullet jumping and croakers making their funny sound. Ed Emmons gave me his class ring there. (It was too big and too heavy for my finger, so I wore it on a chain around my neck until we were married two months later and I got a proper gold band.) That pier was destroyed in the last hurricane, twenty years ago. Blown clean away, not even the pilings left. The town's never built it back, people don't need a place to go on summer evenings, not any more, not with air-conditioning and television.

Anyway, like I was saying, Dr. Hollisher built his pier— a modest, sensible one. For a week or two he was content to put on a big straw hat and sit out there crabbing. Then he discovered boats. The house filled with books and diagrams and plans.

He bought his first boat, a small sailing dinghy. He'd be out all day long, crossing and recrossing the bay, alone, teaching himself from the instruction manuals he brought along. For a beginner he wasn't the least bit timid or afraid. Once I saw him off Goose Pass, way over in the northeast corner of the bay. Since the wind was southwest and building up a nasty little chop, I knew he was going to have a terrible time coming back.

Next morning when I came to work, he was fixing a second pot of tea and he looked very tired.

I said, "I saw you over at Goose Pass yesterday."

"Yes," he said, pouring the water. "Did you notice the wind?"

"You must have been late getting back."

"Slightly after four this morning."

"You could put an outboard on that dinghy, you know, and save yourself a lot of trouble."

"Ah, yes," he said.

But of course he didn't. None of his boats had motors. And he had a lot of them over the years, he kept changing— three or four different dinghies, a Flying Scot, an old Herreshoff. And the others: dory and pirogue. First the pirogue. He found someone who made them in the old Indian way, burning and hollowing a cypress log. He took quite a while learning to paddle that, I can tell you, and spent more time in the water than in the pirogue. Finally he got the hang of it so that he could hop in like a boy and use slow even strokes to skim lightly across the very top of the water.

He sold the pirogue and bought a beautiful little rowing dory. Rowing must have hurt his back, though, or maybe it just wasn't as pleasurable as he thought it would be, because after a few months he no longer used it. He didn't sell it either, just kept it at his dock. It was that pretty. And then he discovered catamarans. His first was small and yellow and white with a silly flower design on the sail; he got it from a Sears catalogue or some such place. He followed that with a battered secondhand Tornado Cat and then a brand-new eighteen-foot Hobie, one with a centerboard in each hull. "I have entered my second childhood," he told me. "I delight in the whistling banshee sound of the rigging as I speed around like a hot-rodding teenager."

It was only a matter of time before he decided that sailing wasn't enough for him. He had to design and build boats too. That's when he met Claude Roberts, who worked as a carpenter at his grandfather's boatyard in Annandale. Old Roberts had started that yard back in the forties and they did a lot of hauling out and repairing, but they weren't builders. Not until Claude came home from the service and got in his head that he wanted to design and build catamarans. He built just exactly two, before his money ran out. They looked like Hobies, only he'd added a kind of little low cabin and called them cruising overnighters. Of course nobody wanted to sleep in such tight little holes, and the catamarans stayed on the beach, only occasionally renting out by the day. That was the end of Claude's career as a naval architect, until Dr. Hollisher came along.

He rented one of the vacant sheds at the boatyard and he and Claude began work on their boat.

After that Dr. Hollisher couldn't seem to think of anything else. Books and plans and blueprints—he'd leave them all around the house, tossed in a corner when he'd decided they weren't what he needed. He didn't seem to care about neatness any more. Each day the mail would bring him more books and more papers. He set up a draftsman's table in his living room so that he could work comfortably at night.

And he just forgot about everything else. He never looked at his camellias, even though he'd spent years on some of the hybridizing attempts. (I tried to keep some of them; I was curious, you know. I got only one bloom and that was pretty ordinary looking.) I don't think he even set foot in the study where he kept his chessboards. Once I moved all the pieces around, just to see if he'd notice; he didn't. And he never touched his radio any more. He even stopped complaining about the antenna. Matter of fact, Belters Electronics was so surprised by his silence that they telephoned one day to see if the thing was working properly at last. Dr. Hollisher still had his card-playing evenings, but you could see that his heart wasn't in it. Occasionally he even forgot to call the caterer about the food for his bridge group, and I had to buy cheese and sausage trays from the grocery, frozen brownies and the like. "Get whatever white wine they have," he said. "We seem to be running low." If they only had Gallo Sauterne, he didn't care. Not any more.

The only important thing was that boat. He had me change my hours and come at eight o'clock so he could get an early start. (He had to wait for me. All the years I'd been there I'd never had a key to the house.) And every morning he'd be waiting for me, walking impatiently up and down. He couldn't even wait long enough to tell me what to do that day; he'd write it out and leave it on the kitchen counter. Sometimes when they worked late, Claude would spend the night, and then I'd have two of them pacing up and down, staring at their watches if I was so much as five minutes late.

Well, after a year or so of that kind of work they finally launched their boat. It was a weird-looking thing, a kind of lopsided catamaran, with hulls of uneven sizes, one little, one big. On the side in large letters they'd painted the name *PROA*, I suppose so people would stop asking what it was, and maybe stop making jokes about the mismatched hulls. *PROA I*, it said, as if they were expecting it to be the first of many.

Like I said, it was a strange-looking boat. The fiberglass hulls were finished so roughly that the whole thing looked fuzzy and out of focus, a bit like a sweater that had started to pill. And the thing didn't sail, at least not very well it didn't. I forget the details, but something was wrong with the steering and with the rigging, and the boat kept capsizing. They worked on it, hard, month after month. They moved the mast and then they shortened it; they changed the rigging and they got a different cut of sail. Nothing helped, nothing worked.

Finally Dr. Hollisher brought it to his pier and anchored it there. Every time I looked out the window I'd see it, and every time I did, I'd think: stray kitten. That's exactly what it looked like. You know how sometimes a stray cat will come to you and have her kittens at the front steps, all dead but one and that one sick and misformed and sure to die in a day or so. . . . That's what the *PROA* looked like.

Claude went back to his old job as carpenter at the yard; he did come every weekend to tinker with the boat (though they didn't try to sail it any more) and take new measurements and draw new plans. Because Dr. Hollisher was planning another boat. There was a file rack on the living room coffee table; the folder headings said Hull Dynamics, Rigging Stress, Function Variables, and things like that. The planning went slowly and finally just about stopped. Claude still came over every weekend, but now he amused himself rowing Dr. Hollisher's little dory up and down the coast, having a wonderful time with it. As for Dr. Hollisher, he went back to his fishing. He still had quite a lot of gear neatly packed away from years before, but none of that would do. He insisted on beginning all over again, with new equipment. He started this time with half a dozen books on fly-fishing and surf casting. He even bought a copy of *The Compleat Angler*, but he didn't finish it. I guess it wasn't practical enough for him. He joined some sort of club and went on a fishing vacation in eastern Canada. When he came back, he took down all his chessboards and set up a long neat workbench. With the help of a book or two, he began tying his own flies. And he spent hours of every day practicing his cast. Over and over, making notes about the equipment and his progress. He was always very thorough.

The time came when I had to tell him I would be leaving. I hated to do it. I knew just how upset he would be. At first you could see that he didn't believe me, then he looked shocked, and finally angry.

"Why? Is it a question of money? Am I so difficult?"

"No," I told him, "I'm going to get married."

"You are going to do what?"

"I am going to be married in November."

"What does this gentleman do—or what did he do?"

It was my turn to be surprised. Dr. Hollisher had never been curious about anything before.

"He's a retired electrical engineer, his name is Alfred Morton, and he spends the winter at the Riviera Hotel. I've known him for four years."

"You are in no hurry to marry? At your age how much time is there left?"

"Quite enough."

He seemed puzzled by the sharpness of my tone; he frowned and hesitated. I was annoyed at myself; he was a very eccentric man but he certainly didn't mean any harm. Trying to be polite, I said, "I met Alfred when he backed into the side of my car at the Sungate Shopping Mall. He lent me his car while mine was being fixed."

"I met my wife in a hospital emergency room," Dr. Hollisher said abruptly. "Her father had just died in a car accident."

I didn't know whether to congratulate him on the marriage or commiserate with him on the funeral. So I didn't say anything. After all, I remembered, the marriage had died too.

As things turned out, I was able to find a wonderful housekeeper for him: Enid Waterson, her husband had a navy disability pension so she needed extra money and Dr. Hollisher paid very well. I went with her the first few times, to show her exactly how things were done, so that there wouldn't be the slightest change to upset him.

I got married. My children were there and Alfred's and all the grandchildren, every one.

Truth is, I'd never liked living alone, I was used to having a man to take care of. Alfred and I got on very well together, our new life seemed to suit both of us. We visited his daughter in Chicago for a month or so in May, then we'd take a long summer vacation somewhere, and by September we'd be back here in my house for the winter. I'd see Enid Waterson at church now and then, and she'd tell me how fine everything was with Dr. Hollisher. And occasionally, more often than I would have expected, I'd see Dr. Hollisher himself—most often in the Sungate Mall, where I'd met Alfred. (We always parked in the exact same spot: a silly old people's joke.) Sometimes Dr. Hollisher would see me and wave, and sometimes he'd be walking along, so busy he wouldn't see me at all. Once I saw him looking at the cars in the Ford dealer's lot and once I saw him coming out of the Main Street Bank, which wasn't the bank where he had his account. And once Alfred and I saw him at a movie. I was just getting up to say hello to him when the lights went off and the film started. When it was over, he was gone. He hadn't stayed for the whole show.

I didn't think of him very much. I was busy. We always seemed to have company coming, people who needed to be fed and entertained.

That last April morning was sunny and beautiful; the first magnolias were blooming, the ones at the very top of the trees. I'd just invited Alfred's youngest daughter to spend the weekend—she'd been visiting her child in college in Florida—and I was wondering what to have for dinner. I'd begun my shopping list when Enid Waterson knocked on the kitchen door. What should she do? she asked. Dr. Hollisher didn't answer his bell, the door was locked and she couldn't get in. (Like me she didn't have a key.) Should she call the police? I said: No, I'll go back with you. So off we went, leaving a note for Alfred, who was just around the corner helping one of the neighbors with plans for a swimming pool.

The back door was locked, just like Enid said. So we walked around the house and there was the front door standing wide open. We tiptoed in carefully, not knowing what to expect. And found nothing at all.

The lights were still on. A book called *Maigret Takes a Vacation* was face down on the coffee table, like he'd just put it there. Next to it, a highball, ice melted and overflowing the coaster to stain the wood. And a chicken sandwich, untouched, the neatly trimmed white bread beginning to dry and shrivel at the edges.

I called the police. They looked for signs of forcible entry or violence, or other evidence left by the perpetrators, so they said. There wasn't any. There wasn't anything missing, not the expensive electronic equipment, not his car, not anything.

After the first excitement, the police seemed to lose interest. Maybe he went off visiting, they said, doesn't he have a family? Yes, I said, a daughter. Well now, they told me, he's just taken it into his head to go see her. Call her if you're worried about him.

But how could I? I only knew that her name was Judy.

I took Dr. Hollisher's address book and called every number in it, starting with his card-playing friends. None of them had seen him since their last game, and they didn't know he had a daughter, he'd never mentioned her. After that I called all the business numbers, the plumber, the electrician, the man who'd repaired the roof last month, the painters, Belters Electronics, hoping he'd said something to them. He hadn't. I called his travel agent, who told me that in just a little over a month Dr. Hollisher was scheduled to go fishing in Colorado. I called the registrars of the three schools he'd attended over the years; I called two professors: one had moved away and the other only remembered something about hybridizing camellias years ago. I called old Mr. Roberts at the Annandale Shipyards; he hadn't seen Dr. Hollisher for months. Young Claude wasn't even there; he'd taken a seasonal job at a Carolina coast resort, they thought.

There was nothing else we could do. I found an extra key (it was neatly labeled in a box in his desk), and Enid and I locked the door behind us.

I went about my business, doing the shopping for dinner. All the same I felt restless and out of sorts: something was wrong, I knew it and I couldn't think of it.

It wasn't until late afternoon that I got my thoughts in order and remembered that something was missing at Dr. Hollisher's house. I closed my eyes to make the picture clearer: I was standing on Dr. Hollisher's front porch, looking off across the bay. I could see the stretch of clipped green St. Augustine grass sloping down to the whitish-yellow sand and beyond it the little pier like thin black lines drawn on the grayish blue water. The misshapen *PROA* was there, wallowing uncertainly in the small swells. The dory was gone.

Alfred came with me this time, and we walked all around

the house, searching carefully. As if a dory could be hidden behind an azalea bush. Eventually we found ourselves standing at the very end of the pier, staring down at the water. It was full of seaweed; the reddish air bladders decorated the surface like faded Christmas holly.

"Well," Alfred said, "that's where he went. With the dory."

So I called the police again and the Coast Guard and told them that Dr. Hollisher and his boat were both missing.

A week or so later they found the dory; a charter fishing boat brought it in. It was five or six miles offshore and far to the west, the way the currents ran. They never found Dr. Hollisher.

Well, that's past and gone now, but it still bothers me, you know. I keep wondering what happened that night. There he was sitting and reading, like he always did. He'd fixed a sandwich and a whiskey with lots of ice. The reading lamp was tipped just right over his shoulder, he had a new detective story. And then, like somebody had called him, like somebody had called a good child to come home, he put the book face down and walked straight out the door and rowed away.

Eventually he was declared dead, and they found he had a deposit box in the Main Street Bank; there was just one thing in it: his will, neat, handwritten, very precise. He left the house to me. "She has taken good care of it for so many years," he wrote, "I should like to think of her living in it now."

Didn't that cause a row. People whispered all sorts of things; Dr. Hollisher's daughter came back making scenes and threatening to sue. Alfred, who was pretty annoyed himself, suggested we go visit his daughter in Chicago. And a cold wet spring we had there too.

Of course Alfred and I never lived in the house. It was bigger and nicer than mine—it had that lovely view across the bay—but I couldn't ever live there. Whatever the law said, it wasn't mine. It belonged to Dr. Hollisher. I knew I'd feel his ghost. And I knew that every night I'd be listening for that same call he heard.

We sold the house to a couple with two young children. I drive past it now and then, just to see. They've painted it a pale pink with black trim, there's a slide where the camellia garden used to be and a swing on the oak tree in the side yard. If they hear anything, those people, they've never said.

Alfred and I put the money in a savings account. We've decided to use it to travel, to go to places we never could have afforded before. Next week we're leaving for Egypt and a trip up the Nile to Aswan. I've always wanted to go there. Ever since I was a little girl looking at maps, I've said: I want to go there.

Now, I'm sure that when I finally get there, when I really do see Cairo and Thebes and Karnak and the Valley of the Kings, everything will be so wonderful and exciting, I'll forget how it was all possible.

But I don't know. I just don't know.... The planning hasn't been as much pleasure as I thought it would be. And sometimes I do wake up at night listening. I still don't hear anything.

And I wonder, maybe I should.

ENDING

By one o'clock the other bank of the small bayou had completely disappeared in the summer night fog. In the muffled quiet, the flock of pet ducks, the five not yet killed by turtles, climbed slowly out of the waterside reeds and plodded halfway up the lawn, to fall asleep abruptly, heads under wings. The lawn, smooth green zoysia silvered with fog like a warm hoarfrost, rose gently to the flagstone terrace of a low curving glass and steel house. Inside, beyond tall mist-haloed windows, lights burned brightly in rooms that were quite empty, except for an occasional white-jacketed waiter, collecting forgotten glasses and plates.

In the service drive, concealed by bushy azaleas, two young men put the last of the band's electronic equipment into a bright red van and, yawning, drove away. Immediately a caterer's truck pulled into the empty space to load neatly tied plastic trash bags. Someone began whistling softly. Overhead a mockingbird answered sleepily.

The wedding was over.

Barbara Eagleton, mother of the bride, sat on the curving stairs in the front hall. Her thin brown face, so much like Diana Ross's, was creased with fatigue. She was trying to decide whether she wanted to laugh or cry. While she thought, she absentmindedly picked bits of food from the stair carpeting and tossed them down to the polished wood floor. Occasionally her fingers brushed irritably at a wide stain on the peach chiffon of her skirt. She hated the smell of stale champagne.

All in all, she thought, the wedding had gone very well—from the candle-lit church to the candle-lit reception. The house looked lovely, everybody said so. The band, brought especially from New Orleans, was marvelous. Her daughter, Solange, had been married surrounded by all the signs of affluence, the sweet glittering softness of money.

Her eyes, trained by years of housekeeping, moved along the hall. The wide cypress boards—ones she'd found in an old plantation house, lovely old boards—were sprinkled with bits of wedding cake, their shiny polished surface dulled with a film of sugar. The Tabriz rug glistened with bits of broken glass, tiny bits like grains of sand, sparkling in puddles of spilled champagne.

In the morning the cleaning crews would come.

It had been a wonderful party, she thought, everything a wedding celebration should be—joyous and lively, floating on oceans of champagne. There had been only a single bad moment, when the youngest Mitchell girl passed out in the bathroom. Her friends quickly revived her with ice packs and hot towels and great whiffs of pure oxygen. (A tank stood ready in the bedroom; Barbara Eagleton thought of everything.) She had come round very nicely with such treatment. When she said a polite good-bye some time later, Barbara noticed that she walked quite steadily, though her Nipon was hitched crookedly at the waist and her eyes had an empty cancelled look to them.

Noisy in the damp night air, a caterer's van backed down

the driveway. And a large tree roach swooped on crackling wings through the open front door to begin delicately eating bits of spilled food.

Barbara stood up, shuddering, took one step toward the insect, then changed her mind and went to the pantry instead. A waiter was packing away glasses. "There's a huge roach in the front hall. Could you get rid of it—I can't stand the things. Just wait until I'm out of the room."

She hurried back across the hall, not looking at the shiny black shape nibbling the sugary grains, and closed the living room door firmly behind her.

"Whatever is chasing you, Barbara?" Her mother was sitting alone in the Queen Anne chair by the window. "I'm just finishing supper"—she smiled at her empty plate—"which is the worst thing I could possibly be doing. My diet will be ruined for a week." She got up slowly, majestically; the stays of her corset creaked audibly. "I've been looking at that picture," nodding toward the painting of *HMS Courageous Liverpool 1879*. "I mean really looking. It's absolutely hideous."

"You gave it to us," Barbara said.

"Yes," her mother said, "that's why it bothers me."

From the front hall, partly muffled by the closed door, came sudden running and stamping, and muffled giggles. "Whatever is that?" Her mother yanked the door open. "My, that roach is giving you quite a chase, isn't it? No, no, don't do that. Don't squash it on the rug."

Barbara fled hastily to the terrace. After the air-conditioned house, the summer night was stifling, the fog a heavy pressure against her body. Its astringent wetness filled her lungs and she coughed, feeling almost panicky. Then the feeling was gone and the night was no more than a usual summer night and the fog only a soft mist that blurred everything pleasantly.

In the corner of the terrace two waiters were searching for glasses in the flower beds; they moved slowly, laughing softly to each other, voices distant and muffled. The lighted swimming pool gleamed a clear turquoise blue in the night. On its surface the guttered remains of a hundred flower candles bobbed and turned gently. And in the center of the pool, in a floating chair, was Justin Williams. His silk tuxedo lapels glistened, his boutonniere was a sharp crisp dot, his sodden trousers and black shoes trailed over the edge of the float. He lay back, totally relaxed, contemplating the glow on the tip of his cigar.

"Justin," she said.

He lifted his cigar to her in greeting, silently.

"I'll get one of the young men to help you out."

"No, my dear, I am perfectly comfortable." He paddled his feet gently. "If you see a waiter, though, you might ask him to bring me a drink."

"Do you really want another drink? Are you sure you're all right? Really?"

"It has been a wonderful party, my dear. And, until the fog came in, the stars were as soft as the ones in Jamaica. Do you remember them?"

"Yes," she said.

They'd met in Kingston years ago—she and her mother on vacation. Barbara was overwhelmed by the physical beauty and the languor of the place; she spent drowsy uncounted days doing nothing. Her mother seemed to come more alive in the heat; she went everywhere, saw everything. She visited ruined sugar houses and thriving coffee plantations, a convent school, an experimental agricultural station, and a bauxite plant. She went to native craft shops and she visited museums. And she met Justin Williams at an exhibition of Haitian paintings. He was some sort of magistrate, Barbara remembered, and a businessman. They had tea, he drove her back to the hotel, he took them both to dinner. Thereafter he became a part of their days, as guide and storyteller, even once taking them home to meet his wife, a beautiful half-Indian woman who was childless.

"Jamaica was wonderful," Barbara said, "especially that first time."

After that her mother went to Jamaica three or four times a year and Justin visited them on all family occasions, like her wedding and the christening and marriage of her daughter. He did not like the United States. "I do not like the presence of so many white skins," he told her once. And he remained her mother's friend, year after year. At times Barbara found herself wishing he had indeed been her father.

"I'd never seen a country so beautiful," Barbara said.

"Ah yes, Jamaica," he said to his cigar. "Even these do not taste the same. Mr. Manley and his government ran me out, yes, and all the people like me. But I have not done so badly, little Barbara, not so badly."

"So I hear," Barbara laughed. He lived in Nassau now, was interested in Florida real estate development. "My mother says you've been very successful."

"Ah." Against the blue pool depths, his dark face hung suspended, motionless. His eyes scanned the terrace, saw no one. "Waiter," he shouted, "waiter." The ducks on the sloping lawn shifted and gabbled. A waiter came at a trot. "Young man, a Scotch and water, please. Water, not soda. My need is great."

Justin Williams let the hand holding the empty glass slip to his side, touch the water. His fingers loosened and rose, flicking themselves dry delicately. The glass sank, wobbling slowly.

Barbara looked down. There were a dozen glasses on the bottom, as well as a bridesmaid's bouquet, paper napkins, a very long orange scarf, and a single shoe with a glittering rhinestone heel.

"Barbara," his soft voice floated through the layers of warm night, "I asked your mother to marry me."

"What did she say?"

He waved his cigar back and forth, a comet against the night. "She said she would never marry any nigger from Jamaica."

"Yes. Well"—Barbara shrugged—"that does sound like her." But why, Barbara wondered, had the subject of marriage come up at all? Why now?

Justin kicked his feet lazily in the water. "A man should be married. It is the way of things. My wife has been dead for two years. I have honored her memory with a double period of mourning, because she was a good woman. But, you must know, I am a married man by nature. I have lived all my adult life as a married man. I intend to be a married man again."

"I am sorry about my mother," Barbara said. "I wish she would marry you."

"There are many women in the world," Justin said slowly, alcohol-numbed. "Many many women. Some of them are beautiful and young, but they are not the sort one marries, not a man like me. At my age blood does not rule the head. But an intelligent woman, a capable woman, a handsome woman, of suitable age, a friend. That is your mother. And she says no."

The coatless waiter returned with his Scotch and water. Justin stretched out his arm—there was ten feet of pool between them.

Barbara got the pool skimmer and with its long pole pushed

the floating chair to the side. Justin accepted the glass and slowly flutter-kicked himself back into the exact center.

He took a small sip. "Barbara, my dear, I have tried to be reasonable. I offered her a marriage contract. I am not a poor man . . ."

"Neither is my mother," Barbara laughed. "If you like, I'll talk to her, but I don't think it will do any good."

"Your father was a Jamaican," he said.

"That's what my mother tells me."

"Ah." A gentle sigh and then silence. He seemed to have forgotten she was there.

A sudden burst of laughter from the kitchen—curious, she went to the open door. Three waiters and her husband, Henry, leaned against the polished steel counters, drinking cans of beer.

"Why, Barbara," Henry said, "I had no idea you were outside."

"Justin is floating in the pool."

"Still? He's been in there for a hell of a long time. Well, not to worry, Barbara. We four shall remove him. Without falling in ourselves, of course." He toasted her with the can of beer. "What shall we do with him?"

"He certainly can't go back to the hotel in that condition."

"Barbara, I had absolutely no intention of depositing him on the Regency's doorstep like a sack of wet laundry to be hauled inside by the doorman and dragged upstairs by bell-boys." A pause. His voice became serious. "Don't worry, Barbara, I'll take care of him."

"Fine." She opened the refrigerator, which was jammed

with white boxes. "My lord, look at all this uneaten food. Such a waste."

"Your mother gave away twice that much."

"My mother . . . Yes . . . Henry, do you know Justin asked her to marry him?"

"In that case we'll pull him out with extra care."

"Mother said no."

"Okay, we leave him in the pool."

"Oh, really, Henry, don't joke like that. He needs help. Where's the beer? I didn't know we had any."

Henry grinned. "Will one of you gentlemen direct Mrs. Eagleton to the secret supply of beer."

As soon as she left, their laughter began again, following her back through the house. In the dining room a thin stream of tiny ants marched across the buffet, down the wall, and into a baseboard crack.

For a brief moment she saw a vision of a house emptied, eviscerated by patient, neatly aligned ant armies, so that by morning the studs stood naked, a skeleton in the rising sun.

Foolishness. That would not do.

She put down the can of beer, took a deep breath, and went about her housekeeping again.

In the front drive, a single paper napkin was crumpled on the gravel. She picked it up, smoothed it to read *Solange and Mike.* I don't like these, she thought, I wonder why I bought them when I think they're tacky.

She crushed it in her fist and walked down the drive to the street, looking, noticing. A car must have backed into the ligustrum hedge, a great many branches were snapped off. And someone had walked through the low gardenia bed. The crushed flowers filled the night with their heavy sweet scent.

Behind her the house waited, perched between silent fog-shrouded bayou and fog-misted street, its lights going out one by one. It was folding into itself, slipping into a doze like all the silent houses around it. Soon the street would be completely empty, except for the patrolling police car, until Mrs. Talbot drove by on her way to early mass. After that, in its regular predictable order, the day would begin. After Mrs. Talbot, at 6:30 to the minute, Mr. Lejeundre would jog past. At 7:10 a small van from Camp Green Meadow would pick up the Henderson children. At five minutes to eight, Mr. Horton's day nurse would drive slowly by, looking carefully all around the neighborhood, hoping to find little bits of gossip to amuse him during the day. (Poor half-blind diabetic, Barbara thought, the only healthy thing about him was his curiosity.) She would find nothing to tattle about in the Eagletons' front yard, only the tiniest whispers of the night's celebration. . . .

Barbara went inside. Her mother was standing in the hall, holding the can of beer and its sodden wrapper. "Yours?"

Barbara shrugged at the white ring on the polished wood table. "I didn't know it would soak through so quickly. Or maybe I've been out longer than I thought."

"You were out quite a while. Watching the moon or some such thing?"

"No moon," Barbara said automatically. "Fog."

"Whatever." Her mother studied herself in the mirror, fingers automatically touching the invisible lines of plastic surgery.

"Don't worry about that," Barbara said. "It looks great. That man took off at least ten years."

"He was expensive enough to be good. You're sure it's ten years, Barbara, not five?"

"Ten." Barbara took a sip of her beer, shuddered. "I don't like beer."

"I wondered why you were drinking it. I thought it was some sort of mother-of-the-bride neurosis. You know, Barbara, I really must lose some weight."

"Go to a fat farm."

Her mother turned slowly, ringed fingers clasping her expensive new face. "Do you think?"

"You know, Mother, find a fat farm that takes elderly black ladies."

Her mother turned back to her reflection. "I have spent quite enough on my appearance," she told herself firmly. "By the way, while you were moon-watching or fog-gazing or whatever, Henry and his merry men got Justin out of the pool."

"Oh dear, I'd forgotten about him."

"Henry said you asked him to do the rescue. . . . Justin insists that he will not spend the night here—he says that it is not proper for a guest to crash at a wedding reception."

Barbara blinked. Her mother had a disconcerting habit of slipping teen slang into her usual precise and proper speech.

"His clothes are far too wet for him to go back to his hotel, though that is a funny thought. Just imagine a tall, very drunken Jamaican staggering through the lobby dripping pool water and reeking of chlorine and cologne. . . ."

"Justin won't."

"No, he won't." Her mother's short crisp laugh filled the hall. (It was, Barbara thought, completely without amusement.) "Justin insisted he could wear one of Henry's suits. And he was so frustrated when he found there wasn't a single one of Henry's suits in this house."

Barbara said, "My husband was very efficient in his packing."

"After a good deal of arguing and shouting, all of them staggered down the stairs again. At this moment Justin is sitting in my car waiting for me. I'll take him home. Then in the morning, I'll send for dry clothes and return him to the hotel in proper condition."

"Why don't you want to marry him?"

Her mother adjusted the collar of her lavender dress. "This color is dreadful, but it did seem so suitable for the grandmother of the bride."

"Why not marry him?"

Her mother's fingers traced the long string of pearls, tapped the large square amethyst that held them together. "And lavender goes very well with this.... My dear, so many reasons. I don't want to live in the Bahamas.... I am far too old to deal with any man.... If he got sick, I would be expected to take care of him.... And most of all, I prefer living alone."

"I'm sorry," Barbara said. "He's a wonderful man."

"Perhaps you'd like him? You'll soon be looking for a husband."

Barbara caught her breath with a gasp that was near a sob. Tears slowly accumulated in her eyes; she blinked them away.

"Now, don't get upset," her mother said. "You know not to pay any attention to me. Oh, never mind, at least I can take Justin away. With the other garbage."

Barbara watched her walk briskly through the house, heavy body on thin rapid legs. Birdlike.

My mother, Barbara thought wearily, my goddamn mother. Tireless, determined, shrewd, calculating, self-contained— Barbara tried all the words and found that they weren't accurate at all. Sometimes she hated her and sometimes she shivered with the strength of her love and her admiration.

Her mother had fought her way from poverty to affluence, bringing her only child along with her, educating, planning, arranging. She had produced an accomplished woman, the proper wife of a successful man. And Barbara knew (when she was being very honest with herself or when she was as tired as she was tonight) that it was precisely what she too had wanted for herself.

Now that the rapid clatter of her mother's heels had vanished, now that her own weary housekeeping patrols had ended, Barbara went into the den, the smallest room in the house, dark-paneled, book-lined. She settled herself, smoothing her skirt carefully, into the largest brown leather chair, braced her elbows against the arms, steadied her head in her palms, and waited.

In a few moments Henry Eagleton sat directly across from her. He put his coat across his knees and loosened his tie.

She said, "You know, Henry, you've always reminded me of Woodrow Wilson."

"So you've told me."

"Especially in a tuxedo."

"Unless Woodrow Wilson got to Georgia, I don't think I can make any claim to his blood."

"It's funny . . ." There was nothing of Africa in his features, she thought; they were north European. Only the skin stretched across them was brown. "Henry, do you remember the paper bag society?" In college a girl was considered beautiful if her skin was the color of a brown paper bag, nothing darker. "The paper bag society would have loved this wedding, there wasn't a single person in the bridal party who didn't qualify."

"Barbara—"

"That sea of brown, like chocolate candy. With a few white marshmallows here and there."

"You've been drinking. I had no idea, absolutely no idea."

"Absolutely no idea ... no, I didn't even finish the beer. I left it somewhere."

"Mama picked it up."

"So she did. Henry, are you going to go on calling her Mama when we've divorced?"

"I hadn't thought about it," he said irritably. "You don't think about your mother-in-law's name when you think about a divorce."

"Well," she said, "I just did."

"Listen ... I've locked everything. I'll leave by the front door so all you have to do is put on the burglar alarm."

"Why don't you do it?" she said.

"Because I'm leaving you my keys. Because I can't keep keys to this house any more."

"It wouldn't be proper," she said dreamily.

"No," he said, "it wouldn't."

"I know, we agreed."

"Years ago we agreed, Barbara."

"For the child. So she could have somebody to walk down the aisle and somebody to sit in the front pew."

"I don't know why you sound like that, Barbara."

"Solange had a beautiful big wedding, we got married at city hall, and my mother never got married at all. And you don't know if your parents were married or not."

His mouth drew tight. "I have always assumed that they were not married."

"It does bother you, doesn't it?"

"You know it does. We have discussed it a dozen times. I will always resent my parents' having a child they were unwilling to keep." A sharp rasp in his resonant voice.

"You have an unusual voice, Henry. Very penetrating and commanding. You should have been a soldier."

"For God's sake, Barbara."

"Mama suggested I might want to marry Justin. Would you mind if I did?"

"You have your own life to lead."

"I don't know that anyone has asked Justin. . . . You know, when I was in high school and we didn't have much money, Mama used to give me her clothes and things. She never offered to give me her husband before. But of course then she got to be so successful I could afford to have my own clothes and my own husband."

"Barbara, you must have been drinking. I'll get you some coffee."

She waved a languid no. Then grabbed the chair arm again; the room seemed to lurch. "I'm sober, Henry. And I do understand. You are going to leave now and go to your new apartment. Into which you have over the past few weeks moved all your clothes."

"Barbara, look . . . We discussed all this, we planned this rationally. . . ."

"Are you going to marry Elizabeth?"

"I haven't seen Elizabeth for a year and a half."

"Oh," she said, "that was the only name I knew."

"I have many friends," he said stiffly, "but no plans to marry."

"Men get huffy when they talk about their women. Even you."

"Now you sound exactly like your mother."

"I think you'll marry again. If she's young enough, you can have more children. I always thought you'd have liked more than one. If they're girls you can give more weddings."

"You are not making any sense."

"Don't worry about it, Henry. You know, it was a beautiful wedding, truly."

"That's what we wanted, Barbara."

"The flowers were fantastic. Mama outdid herself with them."

"Your mother is a very clever woman."

"All white and lovely. I wonder why they weren't chocolate brown."

"Barbara, really."

"When you think about it—Solange has lived with Mike for two years . . . so they probably shouldn't even have had this kind of wedding."

"I'm going now," Henry said.

"I suppose they thought it was amusing."

"Did you hear me?"

"You're leaving, yes . . . Henry, why this particular day? Why did we decide that you would leave after Solange's wedding?"

"There has to be a time," he said. "You have to plan."

"It could have been our twenty-fifth anniversary. That would have been so neat and precise. I could say I was married for twenty-five years. Now I'll have to say I was married for twenty-four and eleven-twelfths years."

"Barbara, there is something wrong with you. I'm going to call your mother and have her come over. You shouldn't be alone when you're acting like this."

"My mother has Justin to worry about. He is going to drip water all over her gorgeous new rug, he is going to collapse on her beautiful Porthault linens, and he is probably going to throw up on them. She can't be bothered with me. And I don't need her."

"I still think I should call her."

"Henry, don't be an ass. Henry, go away."

His face, unusually dark over the white pleated shirt, floated across her vision. "Good-bye, Henry," she said.

She heard the door close, felt the house, empty and quiet now, settle itself at last for the night. She felt a sigh of relief run along beams and floors. She shifted slightly in her chair, making herself comfortable, and reached for the television control. There were late movies on and she watched the flickering patterns intently. She did not turn on the sound. She was content to watch in silence.

SUMMER
SHORE

How can it end,
This siege of a shore that no misgivings have steeled,
No doubts defend?

DONALD DAVIE

For three days the wind had blown from the northeast, dragging black, fast-moving streaks of cloud across a gray smeared sky. In the summer houses along the coast and meadows of Chenier Cove shutters rattled day and night, doors crashed open and closed, chimneys backwinded soot across ceilings, windows leaked in the heavy rainsqualls. Sea gulls massed in the sheltered meadows and waited, rising now and then with a flutter of wings only to settle again, like a sleeper tossing from side to side. In the woods robins and blackbirds huddled under small shelters of branch and leaf; quail and pheasant vanished into the brush; mourning doves sheltered under house eaves, their five-syllable cry floated muted and despairing on the air. The ocean looked grim and battleship gray, stiff and solid.

On Friday of the Labor Day weekend, the last weekend of summer, the wind swung into the west and began dropping rapidly. The rooftop wind indicators slowed their spinning, their dials registered the change in direction and force. By midnight the clouds seemed to turn inside out, and by Saturday morning the sun rose hot and perfect. On the slopes and on the beaches the granite boulders steamed dry.

At Cleo Wagner's house, long strings of bunting rattled up the flagpole halyards to announce her Sunday evening picnic on the beach. She had given this last-of-summer affair for fifty years, she liked to see the family together, children, grandchildren, great-grandchildren.

Her house was one of the smallest and newest on this particular stretch of coast—she had built it for her seventy-fifth birthday, leaving the other house, called the Great House, to be occupied by her son and his family. Her house was also set quite low within a cuplike depression—to protect her greenhouse and garden—but it was situated so cleverly (the architect was married to one of her granddaughters) that its flagpole could be seen clearly by every other house in the area.

Her picnic was a traditional clambake. There'd been a few changes over the years—and she hated them all. Now caterers from Harrisport rather than her own servants dug the pit and built the fire and collected the seaweed. Jeeps brought the tables and the plates and the ice and the wine and beer rather than the ox-drawn carts she preferred. The last ox cart had vanished in the late fifties. She missed them still.

The next morning, on Labor Day, Cleo Wagner closed the door on her summer and started home. The bright bunting still fluttered from the flagpole, six or eight of the youngest cousins carried her suitcases and packages. Her only son waited at the road to wave after her car. From other scattered houses firecrackers rattled off a salute.

Late that afternoon her son, Dan Wagner, locked the doors of his boathouse. He'd spent almost the entire day there, putting it in order for the winter. He would let no one else do it, he would let no one else help. He brought a sandwich with him for lunch, he drank from a nearby creek, wading up from the brackish mouth to the cold sweet water above.

He enjoyed this day, this last-of-season packing and putting away against the winter storms and the prowling animals. He liked the neatness and the orderliness. It gave him pleasure to work and pleasure to see what he had done.

The life jackets were washed and hanging neatly—he would need to buy at least two, possibly three, new ones. He listed that carefully in his spiral notebook, along with all the other small gear—blocks and shackles and sail stops— he would replace before the next summer. The shiny washed hulls of three Sunfish were hoisted to the boathouse rafters, their masts hung beside them. Two outboard motors, cleaned of salt water, sat on high racks, sheets of plastic spread beneath them. Two dinghies were upended side by side, their oars in wall racks next to precisely looped lines, canvas fenders, whisker poles, hooks, gaffs, and swimming ladders. His powerboat, ordinarily at the dock outside, had already gone to the boatyard for winter storage.

The end of summer, he thought, this sound of closing doors. These now, and tomorrow the final slam as he left the house.

It had been a short summer, he thought, as he began the walk back to his house. June was gray and cold and good only for bluefishing. July was stormy. August held all the warmth of the year and ended in a three-day gale. The gardens were ruined. He'd seen rose petals whirling around the house on swirling currents of air, falling like sea wrack on the slopes, flattening themselves like moths against the windows. All the paths and steps were coated and slippery with leaves.

Well, he couldn't count on his guests to wear deck shoes, so he would have to clear up a bit. He stopped at the garden shed and got a rake and a broom.

Katy Wagner swept the veranda and the deck, wiped dry the chairs and the benches, brought out the blue and white striped cushions. Occasionally she stopped to stare across the calm ocean to the hazy horizon. The beach, yesterday crowded with picnickers, now held only a nervously pecking group of sandpipers. And the Atlantic had changed color. For thirty-odd years she'd watched that deep winter color appear after a storm, and it always surprised her. It was so sudden. Like a heart attack.

Ever since Dan had left to see to his boats, she'd puttered about, packing, putting things away, making inventories for the winter insurance. Her sons, their wives and children were gone and there was very little that needed to be done; still she enjoyed touching and smoothing and folding away blankets and sheets and towels. Summer wound down like a clock with slower but still regular intervals.

She put the last of the cushions into their proper chairs as Dan came up the side steps.

"That's done," she said. "We're ready for the last of the summer crowds."

A handsome woman, he thought, still a handsome woman though she was fifty-seven and her wiry curly flyaway hair was completely gray. That pink dress was a good color for her, it deepened her tan and made her look younger.

"I cleaned up the walks," he said. "You know those stone

steps are so slippery we really should do something about them before next summer. They're dangerous without boat shoes."

"Well"—Katy smiled at the narrow granite steps that reached from parking area to porch—"the very first time I came to this house, just a couple of months after our wedding, I slipped on them. And I remember your father standing just about where you're standing now saying we've got to do something about those steps."

Dan smiled. Any mention of his father brought that small smile to his face, even now, twenty years after his death. "You know, every time I straighten up the boathouse for the winter, I think about him. The way he always insisted on doing it, even that last summer when he was sick. So much of that gear is his, his initials on the oars, and that pretty little dory Carter built specially for him, and even the way most of the things are stowed, that was his doing."

It was easy to remember him with affection, Katy thought, that tall, angular man with the monumental ugliness of an Abraham Lincoln. "Sometimes, Dan, now and then, I think I hear him talking and I'm sure he's in the house."

Dan thought: As long as we are here, he will be here. Just as he was for seventy years, ever since that first summer of his life when his father bought this land and built the first house ... As long as we are here, as long as any of our four sons are here ... The boys understood that, he'd explained to them when they were very small, and he had repeated it at intervals through their childhood. They would tell their children, he was sure of that. ... There was beginning to be a certain reluctance, a certain impatience in two of his sons. They came every summer, of course, and they had a wonderful time. But there was something else, something different. ... They came out of respect for him. When he was dead, they would drift to other locations.... And that was very sad. To him this was more than a summer place, a family enclave. It was a fixed point, a firm center for life to revolve around. Winter was filled with change and movement. They'd sold their house when the last boy married; they gave away most of the furniture and took an apartment in town. Now they were moving again: to a con- dominium in a building not yet constructed in a totally planned residential community. Everything would be new, every bit of furniture. Katy loved doing it, she had great taste.... Here nothing changed. She'd never even suggested it. Some of the furniture had been his grandfather's and showed water damage from the great hurricane of 1927, which had twisted off part of the roof. Most of the furniture had belonged to his parents. It was all handsome and com- fortable, and appreciating in value year by year, especially the larger cabinets which had come from his aunt's house in Philadelphia. He liked them all. Sometimes he found himself rubbing them absentmindedly, as if they were pet animals.

He mentioned nothing of this to his wife; he did not talk to her of things that were close to him. He'd never talked to any woman about them, not even his mother. He loved Katy, but he could never explain feelings to her. She might not understand. She might even laugh.

He remained a little shy with her, a little afraid. She was so much brighter than he, so much quicker. He'd met her on a double date her senior year in college. She was presi- dent of the student body, she'd been in the homecoming court, a shiny new Phi Beta Kappa key hung from her charm bracelet. He had finished college and was doing his military service, an army corporal who shuffled papers all day long, fought boredom, and counted the months to discharge. He hadn't called her. He'd thought about it, but delayed. Finally, she called him. He remembered her words: "I don't know when your leave ends, but I got tired waiting. Does a lady ask a gentleman out for a beer?"

He hadn't been embarrassed, he'd been relieved and then rather pleased with himself. They were married six months later.

Thirty-six years ago, time marked by the growth of the boys.

"Everything's ready here," Katy said. "You have any news?"

"Mother got off right on time."

"I heard the firecrackers," Katy said. "I thought she must be leaving."

"I walked over to the lane to wave her off." He sounded surprised—as if it were a new idea, rather than something he'd done every Labor Day since his father's death. "Seemed to be more firecrackers than usual. Josh and Tricia and the Sullivans, I think. Anyway, Mother wasn't driving. She wasn't complaining, but she didn't look too pleased."

"How would you feel if you had to change your ways just because you'd grown old?"

Their insurance agent had called Dan, very discreetly, to suggest that perhaps his mother ought not drive in heavy traffic, after all she was in her eighties, and wasn't there somebody else in her household? Dan's shoulders shook with amusement as he answered solemnly, "My mother doesn't keep a big staff any more, you know, she only has a houseman. . . ." He waited while the electronic voice gobbled relief. "Of course the houseman is a year older than she is. . . ."

Still, Dan managed to convince his mother that a younger driver was needed for the heavy Labor Day traffic. "Of course, Mother, you could wait and go later in the week when the traffic is much lighter."

"This house is unlivable after Labor Day," his mother said firmly. "I have never stayed longer."

So Dan found a driver who was also a part-time policeman in Harrisport.

"Well," said Katy to the empty Atlantic, "she not only has a new chauffeur, she has an armed escort as well."

"I don't think he carried his gun," Dan answered vaguely, turning into the house. The screen door slammed after him.

Rachelle, who did the daily housework, was leaving as he entered the kitchen. She waved cheerfully. "See you next summer, Mr. Wagner." Hurrying down the freshly swept walk, she called over her shoulder, "This day is fantastic!" She stripped off her blouse and skirt, to walk across the fields in a bright green bikini. The clothes swung from each hand like streamers in the wind.

In his mother's day, Dan remembered, the house had been staffed by Irish maids. Every evening after dinner, bathed and dressed in pajamas and robe, he was allowed to watch the sunset from his bedroom. And from that window, the highest in the house, up under the point of the roof, he also watched the four maids walk down the kitchen path to their lodgings half a mile away. They walked slowly, in single file, each in black uniform (their white aprons left folded and hung in the kitchen). With their measured and careful pace they might have been a procession of nuns at vespers. Sometimes in the late evenings when the wind was right, a tiny thread of singing and laughter drifted across the meadow from their little house.

Those maids were gone, replaced by a constantly changing flow of local girls in bikinis. Only his mother's houseman remained from the old days.

The kitchen was clean and bare, with the characteristic sulfur smell of the well water hanging in its corners. Most people disliked that odor. He found it quite pleasant; he missed it during the first weeks in town.

In the refrigerator were three half-gallon jugs, two labeled MARTINI, the other, a pinkish cloudy liquid, DAIQUIRI. On the shelves below were two platters of cheese. And nothing else.

Katy stood in the doorway. "That's an end-of-summer refrigerator."

"Martinis and daiquiris? Pink?"

"They're strawberry daiquiris. Jean Price drinks them and she says everybody loves them."

"Jean Price drinks daiquiris now?"

"She switched a few years ago, she said the martinis were killing her."

"I hadn't noticed." Which was true. Jean and Boyd Price lived a few miles down the coast, summer friends for forty years. He and Boyd had gone to the same prep school. He and Jean had once been lovers. So long ago now, that love made awkwardly on beaches, on the musky-smelling cushions of sailboats. A large tanned woman with hazy pale blue eyes the color of cataracts. A capable woman, earthy and practical, wonderful outdoors, a better sailor than he was. They suited each other well for years. When the attraction faded, they remained friends, good friends.

"Do they still have that awful grandchild with them?"

"The one who's studying dancing? Yes, they're bringing him today. I couldn't very well say leave that ghastly young man home. . . . And who else is coming? Well, the Abbotts, all their guests are gone. And Midge is coming alone, Phil's gone back to town already."

A thin dark woman who lived miles down the coast in Harrisport, who painted and showed in New York and Chicago galleries, who had an unsteady marriage with a very handsome architect who was reported to be bisexual. They hadn't known them very long, only five years or so. Once he had considered an affair with her, she was very willing. Something stopped him. Something his father would have called the old philanderer's instinct.

Katy said, "And the Rasmussens are coming with their guests. We don't know them. And the Howells and the Seavers. And I forgot who else, I don't even remember who we asked. And of course there'll be Elsie and Alice and Blanche."

His sisters, all older, one widowed.

"Did Alice tell you?"

Dan continued staring at the half-empty refrigerator. "I don't think Alice ever told me anything in my whole life except when I was a child and then it was Daniel, sit down, Daniel, be quiet."

"She told me yesterday that she's going to marry Fred Saunders."

He considered taking a drink from one of the labeled bottles but resisted. Never before six o'clock. "Fred who?"

"You met him at that big bash Alice gave in July, there must have been three hundred people. He was there."

"I remember the party," he said. He'd found himself in a corner of the patio with Ellen Donovan, sitting quietly on a low bench overlooking a small noisy brook. They'd not talked long, but when they stood up again, moving on different paths to the bar, Dan knew that he had found his little friend for next summer.

His father's term: little friend. Dan could still hear him saying confidently: No summer is complete without a little friend.

Katy said, "Alice is very happy."

"Good for her. What does the fellow do?"

"He's retired of course."

He was startled, as always. He never remembered that his older sisters had husbands past retirement age. "All right. What did he do?"

"Insurance. He lives in Indianapolis."

"I hope he can afford her." Alice had a passion for building in stone—houses, slopes, courtyards, hanging gardens in which nothing would grow.

"She says so."

He opened the refrigerator again, considering.

It was always the same, this last day in the house, the same empty silent kitchen (empty kitchens saddened him, like a heart that wasn't beating), the same party, with the group only slightly changed from year to year, and finally the same lobster dinner with his sisters.

"We never have lobster in the winter."

"It wouldn't taste the same," she said. "It's part of the summer."

For a moment he saw Ellen Donovan and a large red lobster lounging together on the beach of next summer—he laughed out loud.

"What's funny?"

"All the rules. How we only eat certain things in certain places."

Katy got two unopened bottles of dry-roast peanuts and poured them into pottery bowls. "I'll tell you something even funnier than that. Excepting your sisters and an occasional cousin, we won't see a single one of these people until next summer."

"Thank heavens. Could you stand seeing them all year long?" Again the quiet smile of Ellen Donovan floated across his memory, mocking his words. "I mean," he said more to himself than to his wife, "there are summer friends, that's all."

They came early, not quite six o'clock, the Prices, and the Rasmussens, and the Abbotts, and Midge in floating floor-length pink, and the sisters: Elsie and Alice and Blanche. Down the road, horns muffled by the heavy trees, cars tooted greetings to each other as they drove toward the house.

They always came early to the last party of the summer, Katy remembered, and they always looked a little bit hurried and a little bit like people whose thoughts were far away. Like travelers changing planes, they couldn't seem to sit down, they shifted from one foot to the other, drank too quickly, were elaborately polite to each other.

Marm Rasmussen, whose name was Kyle but who was called Marmalade because of his orange-yellow hair, brought an unopened half gallon of Scotch. He kissed Katy and put the bottle on the bar. "Hope you don't mind, my dear, but I'd rather us drink it than have the locals get to it this winter."

"We can use it, I'm sure," Katy said. "There's always somebody to drink Scotch."

And Irene Rasmussen said cheerfully, "There's not a drop of liquor left in our house, except that half bottle of vodka we always leave for the cleaning ladies to find."

Marm poured his own Scotch, added a dash of water. "Do you remember when Jules built that liquor cellar, all the bottles ordered and numbered and properly racked, with granite walls like a prison. And he thought it was safe just because the door was triple-locked."

A burst of laughter and Dan said, "I remember how sure he was that the lock was burglarproof."

"It's the locked door," Elsie said. "I'll have a daiquiri, please. They can't stand a locked door and they've got the whole long winter to work on it."

"Poor old Jules."

"Stupid ass. More money than sense."

"The locals had a great winter on the contents of that cellar."

"You remember when Jules heard that the people who cleaned him out had been spiking the sacred Pouilly-Fumé with vodka. To give it more kick."

"Pete heard that story over in Harrisport."

Pete said, "I bloody well thought he'd have a stroke. I only told him because I thought it was kind of funny—after all, what's money to him. But I thought he'd drop dead right there and then."

"Maybe he thought the locals would use his crystal, getting the proper glass of course. . . ."

"Poor Jules."

"Jules is a consummate ass."

"He's not here, is he?"

"No, they went back early this year. He said he had to get to work."

"What the hell does he have to do?"

"I think the summer ends just in time," Thad Carson said.

"Or he'd be an alcoholic," his wife said.

And Katy Wagner thought: They've made the same joke

every Labor Day for the past twenty years that I remember and maybe even more.

"Here's to my new house," Thad said. "My God, the daiquiri is pink. I'm bleeding into it."

"Strawberry daiquiri," Jean Price said. "Everybody's drinking them, Thad."

"I'll be damned. I don't move in the right circles."

Katy Wagner said, "I didn't know you had a new house."

"Retiring, love. The doctor said you can't take it with you and you'll be going mighty fast if you don't get out of that business. So I got a pretty little house on a pretty little Florida key with lots of birds to watch."

"Imagine that." Katy Wagner never thought somehow of these people as living anywhere at all during the winter. It was as if they went into storage or hibernation and only emerged after Memorial Day to begin making summer arrangements.

More people came. They crowded through the doors, jabbering. The Johnsons drove their dune buggy along the beach and scrambled up the cliff, bringing a bottle of Jack Daniel's and a wicker basket carefully packed with crackers and cans of pâté.

"Did you see any of the Tyke Races this summer? Those kids are good."

"I was the committee boat for all the juveniles first week of August."

"Vaughn's boy—a Sunfish, you know—broke his mast. Remember that? Snapped it right off a couple feet above the board. So he jerry-rigged a sail and finished the race anyway."

"And Vaughn said: Little sucker's only ten. Wait till he grows up and see how many masts he loses."

"Helen's going back to work. Oh, yes, she is, that's why they left early."

"Rosalie's daughter married that Iranian."

"It wasn't an Iranian, Cissy, it was a Lebanese."

"What's the difference anyway. She's going to live there, can you imagine. Rosalie is just beside herself. First Harold drops dead and then this marriage thing."

Well, well, Katy Wagner thought. This time I don't even know who they're talking about. And I thought I knew everybody on this part of the coast.

She started to check the supplies at the bar, found her way blocked by the crowd. Never mind, she thought, the glasses seem to have ice in them, so somebody brought along an extra bag or two. They're doing all right without me.

She went outside, to the open deck. Directly below was the beach, its shingle rattling with each wave. Ahead was the open Atlantic, endlessly eastward, empty to Spain. The sun was down now and the water had the soft unreal glow of September dusk. Gray, she thought, like a pigeon. Or a maid's uniform—and she burst out laughing at her own image.

My God, she thought, I am the total housewife.

She pulled a dead flower from the leggy end-of-season geraniums and launched it on the wind toward the beach. It landed on the largest granite boulder, a wispy bit of red against the eternal gray.

"Do you always laugh at yourself?"

She turned, feeling guilty to have been caught. "Only by the end of the summer, I think. It's just a touch of cabin fever."

She did not know him. She did not even remember meeting him. He would be somebody's guest, the typical last-week-of-vacation visitor with sunburned cheeks and ears. He was middle height, middle sized, large eyes behind fashionable glasses, and close-cropped curly gray-blond hair that grew low on his forehead like a sheep's.

She stifled her giggles. I really am getting cabin fever, she thought.

He held out his hand. "Somebody pointed you out as mine hostess. I'm Simon Forster. We haven't met so that's why you're having trouble remembering me."

"Welcome to the last day of summer."

"Everyone leaves tomorrow?"

"This group of houses is all family and we leave, I know. Most people do."

"Leaving only the local people."

"And a few retirees."

He glanced down the beach. "It must be bleak."

"I wouldn't try it." He had nice blue eyes, she thought, and there was something very Irish in his broad face.

"You haven't got a drink," he said. "Wouldn't you like one?"

"I'm going right now."

People were standing in the kitchen, opening and closing the refrigerator. They were hungry, though they didn't quite realize it. They would have one more drink and then they would start for home. It was the same every year.

Katy found a jar of Tang and mixed herself a glass of orange juice. There seemed to be no ice left, but the water from the faucet was freezing cold. She added bitters and bourbon from a bottle half hidden by an empty box of Triscuits. There were also some small bottles of ready-mixed drinks: Amaretto Sour. Whoever had brought that?

The Pattersons kissed her good-bye and wished her a good winter. The Rasmussens left. Then the Prices and their grandson. They had been drinking heavily, their skins smelled of alcohol when they hugged her.

The area around the bar was almost empty now. There was a quarter bottle of gin left, and a large salami.

Suddenly there was a rush to the porches, a lot of pointing and asking for binoculars. (They are packed away, she thought, in our suitcases, ready to leave tomorrow.) There was a large, a very large three-masted ship sailing past, quite close to shore. A wide red stripe across the bow identified it as Coast Guard. She squinted to see the name and thought she made out the word *Eagle*.

"Keith, is that a schooner or a barquentine?"

"How the hell would I know. I can tell a ketch from a yawl and that's about it."

"Somebody call the Coast Guard and ask them what their training ship is."

"So pretty."

"The old ships really had something."

"How'd you like to work those sails in a storm, Dan?"

"Those boys are too young to know better."

"I wouldn't set foot on that thing."

They lined the porch, all looking out to sea, their backs toward Katy. She saw a neatly spread pattern of summer people. Bright dresses sharp against deep saltwater tans, skin crinkling slightly with age and exposure, sun-streaked sun-dried hair smoothed neatly, held in place by setting lotions and hair spray. Attracted by the scent, insects floated over their heads in a shifting small cloud, like a halo. And the men—some thin, some portly, most wearing tan slacks and navy blazers, one or two with madras jackets, so outdated now. Only Marcos was different, coatless, wearing a white guayabera and black bow tie.

The fading daylight gleamed on the heavily starched tucks and pleats. He was no longer watching the ship, he was talking, waving his arms enthusiastically, using the mixture of Spanish and Oxford English he so often affected. He looked, Katy thought, very handsome and distinctive and just a bit ridiculous. Like his name: Mcferson Sebastian Marcos. His father had been very eccentric—he'd spent the last twenty years of his life building a monstrous Gothic palace in Easterly Cove. When he died, his son demolished the whole thing, leveled the ground, filled the various cellar holes, and built on the exact same spot a small modern house, three rooms of glass and steel. He lived alone, he did not even keep a dog.

He shifted his position slightly, saw Katy watching him, and waved with a flash of smile. Then he went back to his conversation.

Katy returned the smile. He was a dear man. They had had a very satisfactory affair two summers ago—or was it three, she wondered—but neither wanted to continue. Love was part of that summer and only that one summer. Like fog or rain or chill—each summer had a different character, each could be remembered with fondness and pleasure.

Simon Forster, the man with hair like sheep's wool, said to Katy, "We seem to have emptied your bar."

"Yes," she said, "we expected that."

"The Stanfords told me it was an annual ritual. I'm staying with them, did I mention that? I live in L.A."

"Los Angeles?"

"Correction, Los Angeles. What I wanted to say was this: we're on our way to dinner and could you and Dan join us?"

She shook her head. "We always have our final dinner of the summer—the last supper Dan calls it—with his sisters and their families."

"I am sorry," he said.

"Perhaps we'll see you next year." His eyes weren't really blue, she thought, but green with yellow and black streaks, like a fancy marble. "Perhaps you'll come back, or take a house for the summer."

"I don't think so," he said. "My family's pretty thoroughly West Coast. And we usually take winter vacations."

"We never do. Dan goes gunning in the fall, for sea ducks. And fishing in the late spring, but those are hardly more than a week each time. We still take the old-fashioned long summer vacation."

The last people were leaving now. All together in a group like children on an excursion, they hugged and kissed everyone in reach as they went.

She saw Simon Forster's woolly head move down the steep path and disappear in the crowd.

I like him, she thought. I wonder what he does for a living and if his wife was here.

From the parking area there was the sound of cars starting. A shout. "Watch the wall." Gears sticking. "You haven't got the clutch in! Put the clutch all the way in." Laughter. "Not that way, there's sand that way." Another rasp of gears. Somebody was whistling, clear and perfect: Purcell's Trumpet Voluntary. "If you're going to drive, Keith, I'm going to walk." . . . "It's four-wheel drive, love, but you don't need it here." . . . "Good-bye, people." One by one the cars moved out. "Good-bye, good-bye." . . . "See you next year." . . . "Next year."

After a final wave to the settling dust, Katy filled a tray with dirty glasses and carried them into the kitchen. Then, crouching, she rummaged through the detergents and cleansers under the sink to find a bottle of Laphroaig. She held it up triumphantly. "Half full."

Dan, who was slightly drunk, squinted at her and bowed deeply. "A miracle. How did that get in there?"

"I hid it this afternoon."

"Katherine, you are a clever clever woman."

The faint smell of party still lingered on the porch. They sat in comfortable silence. The ocean had lost all light now, and the sky was almost black, a star or two showing faintly.

"Feels like fog," Dan said.

It was low tide; there was the swishing sound of surf and then the long sigh and rattle of shingle drawing under.

"We always sit out here on the last evening," Katy said.

"Not when it's raining," Dan said. "It was raining three years ago."

"Of course not when it's raining."

"And eight years ago there was a hurricane Labor Day. We sure didn't sit out here then."

"Oh, Dan, you're being silly."

"You remember the trouble I had getting the generator to start."

"But you did."

And their house blazed with light on the blacked-out coast.

Katy said, "Do you remember the hurricane that came during daylight—when would that have been—in the fifties, I guess."

"Fifty-eight."

"The rabbits were all flattened and spread to the ground, holding on."

Dan poured more Laphroaig into their glasses. Neither moved to add water. "Pretty tonight," he said.

"I wonder how many more summers for us."

"Mother is in her eighties and she's still here."

"When the stairs and the slopes are too much for our arthritis, will we build ourselves a little low one-story house?"

He chuckled. "Katy, you do plan ahead."

"Do you want to be buried at sea?"

He chuckled again. "Now I know you're drunk. No, I do not want to be buried at sea. And maybe you better watch the booze, love. You've got to get through dinner."

"Do you remember when Blanche set off the fireworks and one rocket landed in Caleb's jeep."

"I've done this ever since I was a child," Dan mimicked his sister's voice, "of course I know how to do it. . . . Then she fell flat on her face trying to run for the extinguisher. And she just lay there, screaming: 'Fire, fire.' "

"People always drink too much on Labor Day."

A small stray puff of wind blew from the house. "That smells terrible," Dan said, sniffing the heavy moist air.

"Let's see," Katy solemnly counted, "cigarettes and those nice cigars Onslow smokes. And beer. Somebody must have spilled some, I hope it isn't in the rug."

"I smell garlic."

"That big kosher salami is in the window right behind you. The sour vinegar smell is the platter of sashimi Larry always brings and nobody ever eats."

Dan held the bottle up to the dim reflection from the house. "Last drink."

Katy went on itemizing the odors that floated across the porch. "The diesel smell is from Roy's car, he had trouble starting it. And of course there are all sorts of alcohol smells."

"Pine trees." He sniffed.

"Retsina. Somebody brought it, there's a little left. And I smell a bit of mildew and just a bit of camphor from the mothballs in the closets upstairs."

"I'm getting hungry," he said. "Dinnertime."

"All these years." Katy lost the rest of her sentence. Something about memories and people. Something like that.

She stared accusingly at the glass of whiskey. Whatever was it? No matter. Everything was fine. This house, her wooden shell, protected her. On all sides in the fields and meadows her family lived in their companionate shells, following the same seasons, blooming in June and folding, shutters like petals, in September. Always together. Tribal migration. Tomorrow morning cars would form like a caravan of laden camels, with striped beach blankets for saddlecloths.

"Dan," she said, "what do you call the wife of the ranking male member of a tribe?"

"Drunk," he said.

So he knew what she was thinking. Well, that did save talking.

"Let's go to dinner," he said.

They brought their glasses into the house and added them to the clutter on the dining room table. Then, leaving the door wide open for better ventilation, they went down the steps, which were again covered by drifting leaves. Comfortably, silently, holding hands, warm finger hooked to warm finger, warm breath venting peaty clouds of Laphroaig into the salt air, to the last ceremonial dinner of the summer.

HOME

At five-fifteen when Angela Taylor got back to her office, there were six telephone messages waiting for her.

Dinny, who worked afternoons at the reception desk, said, "Mrs. Marshall called twice. She was getting impatient."

"*The* Mrs. Marshall? *My* Mrs. Marshall? God."

Dinny giggled. Mrs. Marshall was old, rich, difficult, and fond of buying and selling houses. Of the fifteen agents at Peerless Realty, only Angela Taylor dealt with her successfully.

"Well," Angela twirled the note in small circles, "she pays my commission, so I don't care. How long has she been in her present house, Dinny?"

"A couple of years," Dinny said.

"A year to remodel, a year to live in it. And now she's getting restless. Maybe I can talk her into selling this house and moving into a hotel while we look for another. That would make it easier on me." She flicked through the other messages, began whistling quietly through her front teeth. It was a childhood habit she had never corrected, and it meant that she was extremely pleased.

Dinny said, "Good news?"

"If this is what I think it is, I have just sold that monster of a Boudreaux place. I'll get on this right now."

In her glass-walled office cubicle, she kicked off her shoes, wiggled her toes against the soft carpeting. Her back was aching—wrong shoes again. She'd just have to start wearing sensible laced oxfords. They looked dreadful, but she was on her feet too much and the days were just too long. . . . She dropped into her chair and fought off the desire to put her feet on the desk—hardly proper office behavior. She rubbed her face briskly; her makeup had worn off, leaving the skin slightly rough to the touch. It was time to go back to Monsieur Raoul for another series of treatments.

She tossed a half pack of cigarettes into the wastebasket; she would take a fresh one tomorrow morning. She always did. She'd discovered that no matter how annoying or stupid a client was, how devious, uncertain, and utterly exhausting, she needed only to light a cigarette, slowly, slowly, and after the first puff consider the burning tip as if it were the most interesting thing in the world—her annoyance would vanish, her calm return. (Even clients seemed impressed by her solemn ponderous movements.) In all this time—and she'd been a successful agent for twenty years—she'd never grown to like tobacco. She needed it, and it became part of her working day, like the pale pastel suits she wore all year round, very smooth, very well-tailored, with never a pleat or a ruffle on them.

She arranged her telephone messages carefully in order of importance. Took a deep breath and began. It was then five-thirty.

"Miss Prescott, please." A pause. "Look, Vicky, just wait for me. I think I'm finally getting rid of the Boudreaux house and I've got to close before they change their mind. I'm running late, I just got back here, and I've got a list of other calls—a good half hour before I can leave. Okay?"

She scarcely waited for Vicky's answer, she was so eager to get on with the business of the Boudreaux property. The old uptown Victorian house had been on the market for two years, it was way overpriced—and now she had a buyer.

It wasn't until she'd finished—all calls answered, details for the Boudreaux transaction settled, Mrs. Marshall put off until the end of the week—that she remembered the edge in Vicky's voice.

Angela paused, hand holding the phone halfway to the cradle. Dear lord, not one of Vicky's moods. Not when things were going so well and she was feeling so very pleased with herself. . . . She remembered that cool edgy voice. . . . Another mood, probably made worse by that hasty phone call.

She shrugged away her annoyance. Vicky was like that—constantly demanding assurance as if she were a child and not a nearly middle-aged woman.

And that, Angela thought, never would change.

She put her shoes back on, grimacing. She was the last in the office; she switched off the lights and set the burglar alarm as she left.

In the parking lot the summer air was still and hot, the fading light an uncertain pale yellow. She hurried to her car, turned on air conditioner and radio, and took her place in the slow-moving lines of traffic.

Vicky was waiting just outside the shop. Over her head, across the entire second-floor facade, a five-foot signature announced *Victoria*.

Angela looked with approval at the large flowing white script. My idea, she thought, and a damn good one. Flash without trash, she chuckled to herself.

There were still people in the shop: late afternoon was

always busy. The last customers often didn't finish until nearly seven, crossing paths with the incoming night security guard.

She'd been right about the location: Angela gave herself another little pat on the back. She didn't usually handle commercial property, but that didn't mean she didn't know a good thing when she saw it. And this location was perfect for an expensive shopping area. She knew it and she worked hard to see that it developed correctly. She even put a lot of her own money into the area—at the start when things needed a push. Eventually she sold out very profitably, so that now the only thing she owned, with Vicky, was the handsome two-story building that housed the dress shop.

Angela brought the car to a stop. Vicky, small, trim, dark, wearing a lavender dress, slipped quickly inside. Bal à Versailles filled the car.

Ever so much the trim businesswoman, Angela thought with a glint of amusement, except for that perfume. Too heavy a scent, too many flowers had died to produce it.

"I thought you'd never come," Vicky snapped. "Another half hour and I'd have called a cab."

"And be deprived of my charming company?" Yes, Vicky was in one of her moods; the only thing was to pretend not to see it, to be flip and casual. "A good day?"

"Average." Vicky wiped an invisible speck of dust from the dashboard. "The shipment from Arnold didn't arrive, of course."

"They're always late," Angela said. "Don't I remember some terrible confusion with last fall's line?"

"You do." Vicky slumped back in her seat and stared straight ahead. "I don't know why I keep dealing with them. They are so impossible."

"Because, luv, you like their clothes, and your customers like their clothes and they pay ridiculous prices for them and you turn a tidy little profit. Which is why you put up with all the nonsense from Arnold."

"Huum," Vicky said. And fell silent.

The flowers of Bal à Versailles were as suffocating as smoke.

Except for a single lamp in the entrance foyer, their apartment was dark. "Well now," Angela said as she flipped the wall switches that filled the rooms with soft irregular patterns of light, "home at last, far from the madding crowd, the bustle of commerce. Now we discover what Madame Papa has left for us to have with our cocktails."

"Angela, why do you call her that? If she hears, she's going to quit and she is such a good housekeeper."

Angela raised her eyebrows. So the silence is over, she thought. How nice of you to make your first words criticism. . . . I was really getting used to the quiet. I really enjoyed whistling and humming to the radio all that long drive home.

But she said nothing aloud. In their fifteen years together she had learned that nothing she could do would alter Vicky's moods. Sometimes she wondered if Vicky herself controlled them. Sometimes she knew she did not, that they were seizures or spasms quite independent of the body they inhabited.

Ignoring the neatly stacked mail, Angela crossed the living room. "I'm having a drink. You want one?" The curtains were closed, and she wondered if she should open them—there was still a bit of soft twilight in the park outside their windows. No, she thought, drink first. "A drink, Vicky?"

"You're not going to open the curtains?"

She reads my thoughts. Angela gave a mental shrug. . . . "Later. I need my drink to celebrate. This was a very good day."

In the small bar the glasses and bottles and ice were waiting. God bless Madame Papa, Angela thought fervently. She filled the largest glass with ice and poured the gin, not bothering to measure. The feel of the bottle in her hand cheered her immensely, as did the small dish of lemon peel. Madame Papa, whose name was Papadopoulous, was a most efficient housekeeper. And, Angela thought, taking the first long taste of her martini, she makes the most marvelous baklava; why didn't I ever have baklava when I was a child . . .

She stopped abruptly and laughed out loud. The thought was so silly, so utterly silly. The kitchen in her mother's house had been staffed by large black women who presided over greasy black stoves that were never cleaned and large black pots whose outsides were crinkled with grease and age until they resembled an alligator's skin. The pots rattled, half-burned wood spoons thumped against their sides, and the kitchen filled with steam and loud voices and laughter. The food was greasy and heavy and delicious. But, she thought, it wasn't baklava.

She waved her glass and laughed again.

"What did you say?" Vicky called.

"Nothing."

"You were laughing."

So shoot me, Angela thought. But she only said calmly, "I was thinking of the kitchen when I was a child." She added more gin and ice to her glass and turned back to the living room, where Vicky was thumbing through the mail.

"Here," Vicky said. "A fund-raiser for Hart."

"For who?"

"Gary Hart. You know, the next President of the United States."

"Ah," Angela said. "Didn't we just go to something for him? Cocktails in the park with little zoo animals wandering around underfoot."

"That was cocktails and only twenty-five dollars." Vicky was studying the heavy card carefully. "This one is two hundred and fifty."

"Good lord," Angela said, "he must really be serious."

"Look at the list of sponsors." Vicky's practiced eye scanned the long list. "At least ten are customers. We'll have to go."

"I suppose," Angela said to the ice cubes, "you are going to sell them dresses for that event and you are going to make a lot more than the five hundred dollars it's going to cost us."

Vicky said, "I'll put it in the book. The twenty-second."

"I suppose," Angela went on ruminatively to her martini, "your Hart-inclined customers see you there and think you are one of them. And your Reagan customers aren't there to see that you are not one of *them*."

"What?" Vicky frowned slightly. "We are going to a Reagan lunch, I forget the exact date, but it's in the book."

"Behold the devious mind of a retailer." The alcohol was filtering into her blood now. A pleasant warmth began in the pit of her stomach and spread upward, washing over her ears like some soft tropical sea. She sat down and kicked off her shoes.

Vicky went on thumbing through the mail, opening and sorting quickly. For a fraction of a second she hesitated over one letter, then with an impatient gesture tossed all remaining ones aside.

Oh, oh . . . Angela watched the quick flip of the small hand, the flash of rings . . . what's this? That letter annoyed her very much. What do we have here?

"Angela, I asked you about the curtains."

"Open them if you like," Angela said, wiggling her toes.

"I was asking if *you* wanted them. I don't. I don't like this time of day at all. The way the light hits the windows and they shine back like blank eyes, like eyes with cataracts. You know that."

"No, I didn't know that. I don't think you ever said that before."

"I hate this time of day."

"A martini?" Angela suggested again.

"I'll get it," Vicky said. "You put in too much vermouth."

"Ah well." Angela lifted her glass and toasted the ceiling. Things were going to be very difficult, but at least Vicky was talking. Once last year she had not said a word for three days. The absolute silence had eaten into Angela's nerves, though she'd managed to maintain her calm indifferent exterior. She'd even considered some kind of record keeping, some sort of cryptic numbers on a calendar. But Vicky might have found it, might have guessed. And that would have hurt her—she thought of herself as even-tempered and easygoing.

Angela whistled at the ceiling, a bit of the Colonel Bogie march. I wonder if I could stand another one of those, she thought, another record-breaking tantrum.

Vicky tossed herself into the opposite chair. She'd made her drink carelessly. Her lavender dress showed a broad pattern of splash marks.

Angela waited for the liquor to soften her mood. Patient, unmoving, almost not breathing . . .

Vicky drank very fast, and at the end gave a little sigh, a tiny sound like an echo.

Angela said, "I had one fantastic sale today. The old Bou-dreaux place."

Vicky stared directly at her, round blue eyes registering no comprehension, no acknowledgment.

"Just about everybody in the office had tried with it and no luck. Then I remembered that couple from Clarksdale— we met them somewhere about a year ago—they talked about wanting to move to town, and they said they wanted a big old house to do over. A period piece, I remember them saying. So I called them and because they have far more money than sense, they bought that ghastly monster."

Vicky's eyes didn't change.

This is going to be quite an evening, Angela thought. And then, aloud, "We have tickets for that experimental theater tonight. Do you want to go?"

Vicky's eyes snapped suddenly into focus. "No."

"It probably isn't very good." Angela kept her voice even and toneless. "Let's have dinner downstairs at Paul's and then come home."

"I have been to Paul's so often I know that menu by heart. I know how every single thing is going to taste before I taste it."

"When you live in a building, you tend to eat downstairs fairly often because it is so convenient."

"I hate it."

"Well now"—the smallest trace of anger appeared in An-gela's voice—"I certainly don't feel like fixing supper here. I think I'll go to dinner and then have a look at that foolish play or multimedia presentation or whatever they call it."

Vicky's eyes glittered and changed, sparkles like tinsel appeared in the blue irises.

Her eyes were so damned expressive, Angela thought. They showed hurt too clearly, you could see the blood of invisible wounds. Faced by their pain, Angela retreated to the pantry for another drink. Deliberately, measuring carefully, she fixed the martini, tossed both lemon and olive on top the ice. Still elaborately casual, she sauntered back, stopping to pick up the mail Vicky had tossed aside. On top, with its clear printing, its elaborately scrolled capitals, was a letter from Angela's daughter, Louise. Why had that upset Vicky?

The paper crackled loudly in the silence as she smoothed the folded sheets. "Your glass is empty, Vicky. Why don't you have another drink while I read this."

Angela was not sure how she felt about her daughter, that beautiful young woman who seemed capable of endless understanding without a hint of malice or anger. She'd adjusted to her parents' divorce, had lived happily with her father, had grown to love her stepmother. With Vicky, she'd been quietly friendly, relaxed, and quite free of embarrassment. Cool, disciplined, well organized, a model student in college, now working on an MFA, she was married to an associate professor of economics who looked like a young John Wayne.

Perfection, Angela thought. How could I have produced anything so damn perfect. . . . And where was Vicky?

She was standing at the refrigerator, one finger rubbing a small circle on the door. Carefully Angela put her arms around her. In the softness of that body and the muskiness of that hair, Angela felt again the familiar rush of pain and love and tenderness. And something else, something darker and stronger. Something she could not name, something she refused to think about, a force that gave a restless desperation to her life.

Wearily, for the uncounted thousandth time, Angela pushed back the thing that crouched waiting in the shadows. She heard the crackling of its voice and the swishing of its tail. Not yet, she told it, not yet. Not this time.

And softly into Vicky's ear, pink curves under wisps of black hair, "We're both tired, honey. Come on, let's finish our drinks now. I saw some kind of dip in the refrigerator. And after a while we'll go and have dinner at Paul's, but we won't try the theater. Not tonight, when we're both so tired."

Vicky nodded silently, eyes closed, anger lines fading from her small face—the wistful, heart-shaped face that had haunted Angela ever since they first met, years ago, when Vicky was a college student, Angela a young matron with a husband and child.

Now again, as always, seeing Vicky's face close up, seeing the perfect porcelain skin, the lash-fringed eyes, naturally shadowed as some Irish eyes are, the thin-lipped and very small mouth—the face of a mannequin—Angela was reminded again of the toys of her childhood, the dolls whose china heads she had smashed open against rocks just to see the glass eyes spring out and roll away.

Dinner was pleasant. They knew a dozen people in the restaurant, they waved to them. The Bartons, their neighbors down the hall, joined them in the bar for an after-dinner brandy. It was the sort of evening Angela liked best—lively, amusing, time filled with people who were not close to you. Nice people, people you liked, people who were gone before they became tiresome.

Vicky's moodiness vanished. She talked gaily with the Bartons, laughing at their long stories of misfortune and confusion during a trip to Hong Kong.

By eleven they were home. "Huuuu." Angela closed the door and leaned against it. "I am tired!" She stretched, rubbed her eyes. "Bed is going to feel so good."

They had separate bedrooms now that the first frenzy of love had passed and they no longer required a presence within arm's reach all night. Angela shook her head, still puzzled by the lust of those early years, the rhythmic beating of blood that silenced everything else. They had been, she thought, more than a little crazy.

Eventually balance and control had come back. Or was it weariness? Angela yawned. Age and habit finally muffled everything, that was sure.

She ran her bath, poured in oil, and eased herself into the slippery tub, sighing with comfort. These pleasures were becoming more and more important to her—the perfumed hot tub, the wide bed all to herself, the smooth cool sheets with their embroidered edges.

She soaked, half asleep, remembering the first time she met Vicky, fifteen years ago. It seemed even longer than that, all the figures were fuzzy and out of focus, softened by time and distance.

It was a Thursday. Angela and Neal always went out to dinner on Thursday. Their ten-year-old daughter stayed with the housekeeper, Felicia, a thin pious spinster who left the house only for early Sunday mass, who never touched the television, and who turned on the radio only for the evening rosary in Spanish. All her salary went into a savings account. One day she would return to Guatemala and start a shop, a fabric shop that also sold candies and baked goods, she told Angela. But years passed and Felicia did not go home. She seemed to have forgotten her plans. After the divorce she stayed with John and the child. When they moved, she went with them. She was still there; Louise's letters mentioned her occasionally: "Felicia, dour as ever."

On that Thursday night fifteen years ago, the night her life changed, Angela and her husband had dinner early and went to the University Theater for a production of *The Glass Menagerie*, directed by Neal's sister. Angela was bored: the actors were painfully amateur, the staging was awkward. Still, remembering Neal's sister, she applauded dutifully and smiled and tried very hard to be encouraging. Afterwards they went to the cast party in the student center, where they hugged and kissed everybody and laughed loudly and made silly toasts in beer. And Angela met Vicky.

She remembered the exact moment she first saw her—a jolt, a shock. Too violent to be pleasant. (Vicky remembered it differently: "I didn't notice you until you spoke to me, Angela. And then I thought you had a lovely voice.")

Angela remembered it all—the way the room smelled: beer, dust, sweat, the sourish odor of makeup, the sweet smell of cold cream. Somebody broke a confetti egg against the roof and bits of colored paper whirled in the air like bright midges. Neal and his sister were at the bar filling their mugs, laughing and talking as they worked their way through the crowd. A group of student stagehands in T-shirts and blue jeans gathered in one corner, fifteen or twenty of them, stretched on the dusty floor, perched on the windowsills. Vicky was there. She was standing in the bewildered way that was so characteristic of her, hands limply at her sides, a small frail figure in large overalls, dark hair cut short in fashionable imitation of Mia Farrow. She seemed utterly alone in the midst of the crowd.

Angela walked briskly across the room and touched Vicky's

sleeve. "I feel that I know you," she said. "Isn't your name Vicky?"

"No," Vicky said.

"It should be. Vicky Prescott."

"It's not."

"It is now," Angela said. "I just gave you a new name."

Three months later they moved into a small apartment near the campus. Angela took four suitcases of clothes—nothing else—with her.

When she told Neal, he said nothing, absolutely nothing. His face froze, then gradually drained of color until the bones showed as dark shadows. His lips turned white and then a clear pale blue. Without a word he went upstairs into the bedroom and locked the door.

Felicia said he stayed in the room all that day, and there hadn't been a sound. The morning of the second day he appeared at breakfast, he read the paper and talked with his daughter; he asked Felicia formally to stay on as housekeeper, and he drove the child to school. She was delighted; usually she took the bus.

A year later, to the day, Neal sued for divorce. Angela did not contest child custody, finding that weekend afternoons with her daughter were quite enough. She and Neal met occasionally at lunch to agree on the details of the dissolution of their marriage. "You know I have quite enough income of my own," she told him. "I do not think I should ask you for anything."

He nodded gravely. (He seemed to have become very ponderous and solemn, she thought.) "When will you come to the house to select the things you want to keep?"

She shook her head.

"Things of sentimental value? Things from your family?"

"There is nothing," she said. "Nothing at all."

Three years later Neal moved to the West Coast, to begin his own consulting firm. Angela supervised the packing and the moving. And declined again the offer of furniture. Neal kissed her good-bye on one cheek, her daughter on the other. (Vicky had not come, she had always refused to meet Neal.) Then they were gone, astonished at how very simple and easy it all had been.

Six months later there was a formal announcement of Neal's marriage. After that, from a distance, Angela saw her daughter through the rituals of growing up—birthday presents, summer visits, graduation presents, wedding presents. All conducted quietly and factually and coolly, like the business transactions they really were.

Drowsy and comforted by the warm perfumed waters, Angela left the tub, toweled carelessly, reached for a nightgown without looking at it. She patted the heavy embroidery on the edge of the sheet once or twice and fell into a deep black sleep.

When Vicky slipped into her bed next to her, she scarcely stirred. "Tomorrow." She pulled away. "Vicky, it's late and I'm tired."

"I don't want to make love," Vicky whispered so close to her ear that her breath tickled unpleasantly.

"You can't be this spoiled," Angela muttered. "Go away."

"I have to talk to you." There was that rasping note of decision in the soft voice.

Oh, oh, oh, Angela thought in her comfortable sleepy haze, I hope this isn't going to be one of Vicky's long rambling middle-of-the-night talks. "I'm dead tired, Vicky. You can't be this selfish."

"I have to talk to you now." The small voice was cool and steady.

Well, Angela thought, maybe it won't be such a long talk. . . . She rolled over, reaching for the lamp switch. Vicky's hand closed over hers, stopping it.

"No. I want to talk in the dark," Vicky said. "I always talk better in the dark."

"You always talk longer in the dark." Angela squinted at the green dial on the clock: three-fifteen. "I've got a nine-fifteen appointment, and just look at the time."

"Now," Vicky repeated.

Angela sighed deeply, pulled the pillows up behind her, and settled back against them. For a moment she dozed— then shook herself awake. Vicky remained curled in the middle of the bed.

"My dear," Angela said, stifling a yawn, "this had better be important or I am going to be perfectly furious with you."

"I want a child," Vicky said. "I want to get pregnant."

In the silence a far-off clock ticked steadily. A police siren waved a thin finger of sound down a distant street.

"That is important," Angela said dryly.

Vicky was silent, unmoving.

"Is there anything more you want?"

A small despairing hiss, like air from a balloon. "I knew you'd misunderstand."

"You must give me a moment," Angela said, "to catch up with you." (Is this how Neal felt when I told him—when the unthinkable happens?)

"I knew you'd be angry. . . and I knew you'd misunder-stand. I've been dreading this so much that I've been putting it off and putting it off. For months. I just couldn't tell you."

"You have lost your mind."

The bed moved slightly. Vicky was shaking her head. "I don't want to want a child, you see. I know it would be trouble, and I thought you might even leave."

Did you? Angela thought. I don't believe that.

"It got so bad, I even began going to a psychiatrist."

"I didn't know."

"I thought at first it would go away, so I waited. But it didn't. I thought about a tranquilizer or an energizer or lithium if I was really crazy."

"A strange pharmacopoeia," Angela said into the dark. "Was the shrink any help?"

"No drugs," Vicky said sadly, raising her head slightly so that she showed briefly as a silhouette against the pale yellow wallpaper. "He said it would be months or years before anything could change. If then."

"No help from him."

"No," Vicky said.

The clock was still ticking, but the siren had vanished. The room was filled with a faint humming, the building's air-conditioning system. Like the far-off hum of bees, Angela thought. There'd been hives on her family's summer place in Maine.

Vicky was talking again, rapidly, slurring her words. Angela noticed the heavy smell of brandy. She'd been drinking, and she probably hadn't been to bed at all.

"I didn't want you to be angry. I tried every way I knew. But nothing helped. It's even getting worse."

"The urge to procreate."

Vicky sobbed softly.

Dear God, Angela thought, if I still believed in you, I would think that you are punishing me for my sins. But I left Sunday school too long ago for that. . . .

"You've got to understand," Vicky said. "You've always

helped before. Even when my parents died. You were so kind then."

They'd been killed in a highway accident and Vicky, wild with grief, neither ate nor slept. Finally Angela took her, dizzy with Librium, for a six months' trip through Europe. They worked their way page by page through the points of interest listed in their Baedekers. They climbed mountains, hiked through forests, they exhausted themselves in the thin Jura air and staggered through the smells of Naples.

"Listen to me now." Vicky spoke clearly and slowly, as if she were instructing a child. "I am thirty-six. How much longer can I have children. One child. I feel, I don't know, I feel hollow and empty and useless. Sometimes I feel so light I think the wind will blow me away."

"It won't," Angela said.

"You have a child." The harsh accusation startled Angela. "You have a child. Every time a letter comes from her, every time she telephones and talks to us, I want to die. Because I have nothing."

Nothing, Angela thought dully, sadly. You have me. And your career. You are the owner of a very successful shop. You have friends. You have a lovely apartment. And just today I saw a carriage house uptown, not too large, early nineteenth century, with lovely cypress woodwork, and a garden that is completely enclosed by a high brick wall, a perfect house for us. And you have love.

"Nothing," Vicky repeated as if she had heard.

"I'm going to get a drink."

"Take mine." Vicky put her glass carefully into Angela's hand. "I want you to understand, but I'm not saying it very well."

"I understand," Angela said.

"No," Vicky said. "I love my life. I love you and I love

my work. There isn't anybody else, you know that. I make more money every year. So it isn't any of the things it's supposed to be—not sex, not money, not boredom."

"That what the psychiatrist said?" Angela drained the glass, almost choking on the straight brandy. She hated drinking like this, in a race for comfort.

"Not exactly, but I guess so, really."

"Look, Vicky." Angela tried to put the glass on the night table, missed in the dark, and heard the glass roll across the rug. "It's late, we have to work tomorrow. Why don't we both come home early and have a sensible discussion."

"No," Vicky said. "I know what I'm going to do."

"Get pregnant?"

"Yes." The darkness and the small voice and the absolute determination.

I am angry, Angela thought, I am white hot and frozen with anger. "You seem to have thought it out. Have you decided how? I mean, you are an attractive woman, you can certainly find a man. You could even shop around until you found a man whose face you'd like to have repeated in a child."

A small sigh. And silence. Vicky was not going to be lured into an argument.

"I suppose," Angela went on, "you could always have it done artificially. Like a cow."

This time Vicky was silent so long that Angela thought that she had fallen into a drunken sleep. Her own eyelids strained in the confining dark, dry and aching.

Eventually Vicky said, "At least then my bones and blood will be quiet."

"Just what I always wanted: quiet blood." Angela bounced out of bed, went to the pantry. She poured a large brandy, noticing that the bottle was almost empty. I ought to get out, she thought, I ought to take the car and go for a long drive and just keep driving around until things make more sense to me.

But she didn't. She went back into the bedroom. "Time's winged chariot."

"It's like being thirsty," Vicky said. "You have to have water."

"Brandy. Do you know how much brandy you've drunk? The bottle is almost empty."

"To give me courage," Vicky said simply.

And there it was, the tone, the motion, the gesture that ended all discussion, all argument. Why am I like this, Angela thought, why can she always do this to me. . . . Why does she turn me around? Why can't I leave, even for a drive. Is there so much of my life invested here?

"You are proposing that you and I raise this child together?"

"Yes," Vicky said. "At first I thought you might want to leave, but now I don't think so. I think it will be all right and you will love the child because it's half me."

"Jesus Christ." Angela made another trip to the pantry to empty the bottle of brandy into her glass and top it with soda and the bits of ice that remained in the bucket. The clock there said four-thirty.

Vicky uncurled and lay stretched crosswise on the foot of the bed. Angela sat down Indian-fashion to keep from touching her. "All right, Vicky, we'll raise the child together. If that's what you want."

Vicky's voice was thick with sleep and alcohol. "I knew you would."

"How the hell could you know that?"

Vicky stretched and prepared to fall asleep where she was. "I knew."

Do you know how much of my life I have invested in you? Do you? You, a small arrangement of bones and skin and flesh and blood that I would kill if it would free me. But it wouldn't.

Vicky lay so still Angela thought she had fallen asleep. She got up slowly, carefully, not to disturb her, and began tiptoeing toward the door.

Vicky said clearly, without the slur of alcohol, "You're going to love the child. And I'm going to come to hate it."

"Go to sleep, Vicky." And stop talking, let me alone for a while anyway. Before something I can't imagine or control happens . . .

"You're going to love the part that's me, and I'm going to hate the part that isn't you."

"Vicky, you are terribly drunk. You're not making sense."

"I want your child," Vicky said. "A child that's you and me. Now tell me why that's so stupid."

And with a slight movement and a small sigh, she turned face down and fell asleep. The mattress moved softly with her sudden increase in weight.

Angela went into the living room. She felt strange and detached and very calm. She opened the curtains and stared at the city that stretched beyond the pale reflection of herself. She raised an arm, saluting herself in the imperfect mirror. She was breathing regularly and slowly, all anger and fear were gone. But the moving arm didn't belong to her, nor did that figure reflected distantly back to her.

Traffic flickered slowly through the leaf-obscured streets, lights were beginning to show in some of the distant hill houses, it would not be long until daylight.

She sat at her desk and began a note to Mrs. Papadopoulous, saying that Vicky was not to be disturbed, no matter how long she slept. She herself would call the shop to tell them that Miss Prescott would be late, if indeed she came in at all today, please do not call, any decisions can wait until tomorrow.

She watched the sky. Despite the brandy, she was not drunk, she wasn't even tired. Her mind moved lightly, decisively, thoughts clicking like high heels on marble.

When the first gray morning streaks showed, she would make coffee and scramble a couple of eggs. She would shower and dress, and go to her office earlier than usual. She would finish the paperwork there and then she would make an offer for that uptown carriage house, whose small walled garden would be a lovely safe place for a child to play.

FLIGHT

"There's nothing you can do?"

"We are fairly sure now that the primary site is the liver. That's somewhat unusual."

"But you can't help her?"

"I am sorry. There is nothing at all we can do."

"I'll go home now, Michael. It's time."

"Mother, why not wait a bit longer?"

"Tomorrow, I think. I'll go tomorrow."

"It's a long flight."

"It was just as long when I flew here to visit you, Michael."

"You were stronger then, Mother."

"There was more time then, too. Or I thought there was. Will you see to the tickets? I'll go back the way I came, that flight through Dallas."

"Mother, please wait until you are stronger."

"I will not get stronger. You have talked to the doctors. And I know they are right."

"You could stay here. We are all here."

"I will take the plane home tomorrow, Michael. . . . Now I am sleepy. . . . Is it raining outside? I hear rain very clearly." Water: whispering, giggling.

She, the small child, waited for rain, watched across Mr. Beauchardrais's pasture as the clouds gathered, black and silver. Heavy clouds with ball and chain lightning dancing between them, silently. The spiky clumps of pasture grass faded to pale yellow, glimmering, reflecting like water to the sky.

She sat in the porch corner, wedged comfortably against peeling boards which were corded like the veins in her mother's hands, her father's arms. Sometimes she even imagined that the house's blood flowed through those raised twisting networks in the wood.

Mouse, people called her for her habit of sitting silent and still in corners. And Doodle Bug for the hours she spent under the house, crawling between the low brick foundation pillars, creeping cautiously through broken glass and slate to settle comfortably, flat on her back, at the center of the house, where the damp air smelled of mildew and tomcats and a heavy sweet stickiness that was the breath of the ground itself. . . .

While her mother's feet thudded up and down across the boards overhead, she lay on her back and watched the spiders weaving thick gray webs around the water pipes. Watching for the Black Widow, small with a single red dot on its stomach. . . . When it rained, neighborhood dogs and cats sheltered under the house, politely, deliberately ignoring each other. Huddled against the underside of the front steps, a calico cat fed her latest litter while two dogs slept, twitching and yelping in their dreams. . . .

She sat cross-legged on the porch where the sun-bleached wood was so hard her small pocketknife could barely scratch a mark. She had to be very careful; if her parents caught her testing the strength of the boards, she would get a paddling for sure. As if the boards were something to be guarded, as if they were worth anything at all . . .

She watched the rain. It began with a yellowish kind of darkness in the air, then a shiver while leaves rushed into the neatly swept hard clay yard and spun in rising circles. Just like the cartoons she saw on Saturday afternoons, when her mother had extra money to send her to the movies. (On good days her father walked to work and saved his carfare in a jelly glass on the kitchen counter. For her.) When those cartoon characters ran, they left swirls of motion behind them like the wind and the dead leaves.

Rain meant her father rode the streetcar and no extra coins went into the kitchen glass.

She settled back—no movie this week, that was for sure—and waited for the rain.

On the tin roof, drops tapped, then knocked, then rattled like hailstones. A whispering, a hissing ran along the roof gutters to the cistern at the corner of the house.

Her mother called loudly, "Willie May, come quick. Come help me."

In the backyard her mother was putting chicks and ducklings into the poultry shed. Willie May hated to touch them—the small bony bodies felt skeletal and evil in her hands. She held her breath as she hurriedly put the small blobs safely under shelter. They were so stupid that they would stand in the rain, gawking in curious confusion, and drown.

Afterwards, back in the porch corner again, wet clothes

plastered tight to shoulders, nostrils filled with the scent of her own dripping hair, she watched the air turn smoky gray. She sniffed the sweet moisture-laden dust and occasionally, after a close crash of thunder, she could smell the sharp, nose-tickling odor of ozone.

Another time her mother called her. That once in September during the hurricane season. "Willie May," her mother cried, voice shaking with fear and pain, "Willie May, help me." The child she was carrying was born too soon, a small hairy boy who gasped a couple of times and was perfectly still.

Willie May ran off into the rain, hiding in the heavy tangle of titi bushes and myrtle trees on the other side of the street. She shivered all over—not with cold, because it was September and very warm, and not with fear of the weather, because though the winds were high they were not nearly hurricane strength. She huddled against the trunk of a big wax myrtle, and rain and leaves and bark pelted down on her. Her arms and hands twitched, like a puppet, her body shook so hard that she could scarcely breathe. Perhaps she'd even stopped breathing for a while, because she found herself lying full length on the ground, one ear and eye pasted shut by soft oozing mud.

It was still raining hard and the sky was darker, not with the greenish dark of a hurricane, but the gray dark of night. Looking out carefully from her shelter, across the empty ground, she could see that all the lights in her house were on.

She went home then, because she had no other place to go. The deep gutters on each side of the dirt street were filled to the top (crawfish would like that, she thought), the water was ankle deep on the three loose boards that served as a bridge to her house. She inched her way across, carefully. The boards shivered and quaked, about to wash away. In the morning she would have to go hunting for them and put them back in their place. She'd most probably find them near the Duquesnay house where the ground rose just a bit. An Indian mound, people said, and children frightened each other with stories of walking ghosts.

Out of the darkness her father said, "Willie May."

She hadn't known he was there. His voice came from the dark corner of the porch by the living room window. She stared, dazzled by the bright square of light, saw nothing. Mosquitoes, attracted to the moisture of her eyes, swarmed on her, and she blinked rapidly.

"You ran off," her father said, "when your mama called you. You left her and the baby died."

She wanted to say: I didn't kill him.

But no sound came out.

"Your mama knew you were afraid when you saw the baby, but she thought you'd know enough to run to Rosie's house."

No, she hadn't thought of that. Never once thought of running the three blocks to her Aunt Rosie's house and telling her. She'd thought of nothing but digging under the weeds and the bushes, hiding. Like a mouse gone back to earth.

I'm sorry, she wanted to say.

But again no words.

The water-washed boards suddenly shifted sideways and she fell into the muddy night-black rushing water, coming up coughing and choking, crying with fear, scrambling up the bank of the ditch to the firm hard-swept mud of the front yard.

Her father did not move. She would not have known he was there, except in the quiet night she could hear his breathing.

"Mother, please stay. You're comfortable here and the doctors are so good."

"I do not need doctors now."

"Mother, listen. We only want to take care of you. Don't you understand. We love you."

Oh, I understand. The trap. The trap that caught my father and my mother and even me. But that was years ago, not now. No more love.

She would run away again. Only, when she went to earth this time, it would be for good. And she would choose her own spot.

"The baby didn't die because of you," her mother said.

But Willie May knew better. She knew.

"He died because he was born too soon. If I hadn't strained and fought with that window because the rain was pouring in, and if the window hadn't been stuck . . . He wasn't your fault. But you shouldn't have run away."

She hung her head and the old guilt and disgust settled in her stomach while her chest ached so much that she thought she too would die.

"Your duty," her mother said, "you don't ever run away from your duty to your family. Not ever. Not until you die."

Willie May thought wearily, and with horror: You aren't

ever free. Something always holds you, stops you, brings you back.

"Good evening, Mrs. Denham. Will you have your sleeping pill now?" The night nurse: round black face under a round white cap.

"You still wear your cap, Nurse. None of the others do."

"The hospital doesn't require it any more, Mrs. Denham." She had a habit of repeating the patient's name over and over again. Perhaps she had been taught to do that. "But I worked hard for this bit of organdy and I intend to keep on wearing it."

"I know what it is to work hard for something."

"Yes," the nurse said.

Then there were the usual little night sounds: rubber-shod feet thudding ever so softly, and the soft silky whispering of nylon-clad thighs moving up and down the halls.

I did not come for this, she thought dully, I came to see my son, my only son who lives a continent away in a house with green lawns and dogwood blooming outside the windows, who has two sons, his images. I came to visit and I broke down on the road like an old car.

She could smell the sickly sweet stench of her own skin. Her whole body had an aura of decay.

The smell reminds me of something. Something years ago. I was young, but my skin still carried this smell.

I have only to live until the morning. It is time.

Time had so many different patterns. After her father died, when they were very poor with only his small pension to support them, Willie May went off to work at the Convent of the Holy Angels. Thirteen, tall and strong, and afraid. For three years she lived in a maze of echoing halls that smelled of floor wax and furniture polish and a laundry that smelled of steam and bleach and starch for the stiff white coifs and wimples the nuns wore. Three years of small hard beds in tiny rooms. Of weariness and sick exhaustion. Of prayers and echoing Gregorian chant. And a great emptiness. Occasionally in the garden as she swept the covered walkways, she could hear children shouting as they walked to school. She envied them and their living fathers whose hard-earned money sent them laughing along the sidewalks.

Eventually her mother remarried, a police sergeant named Joseph Reilly, a widower nearly sixty. "Hello, Willie May," he said, when she came back from the convent. "I married your mother." "Okay," she said. He smiled then, and it was settled.

He liked to cook, and despite his name he cooked Italian style. Her mother was beginning to grow fat on spaghetti and sausage and peppers, all glistening with olive oil.

He was a quiet man who spent every evening at home listening to the radio, sitting in his special chair (one he had brought with him to her mother's house) with his feet propped on a stool. He was a kind man and treated her like his own child. Each birthday he bought her a pair of white gloves to wear to church, and every Christmas he gave her a box of Evening in Paris cosmetics, blue bottles held in shining white satin.

There was no talk of her returning to school, the time for that had passed. On her sixteenth birthday she went to work at Woolworth's, at the big store on Decatur Street. She sold potted plants and stood all day behind the counter near the front window, and when she wasn't busy she watched the street outside. The cars and the big delivery vans and the green streetcars rocking unsteadily past on their small clacking iron wheels. Women in print dresses and hats, breathless and harried from the excitement of shopping. Office messengers with brown envelopes and packages and long cardboard tubes. Girls in navy blue school uniforms, arm in arm, and boys gathered at the corner by the traffic light. Bookies and numbers runners whose territory this was; she grew to recognize them and smile, and they lifted their hats to her in passing.

As she watched she felt her quietness and her loneliness slipping away. She felt herself become a part of things, no longer a child looking in, but an adult and part of the busyness and bustle that was life. Her hands, broadened and thickened by the convent work, their nails clipped very short and square across, grew soft and slender, and she filed her nails into careful ovals. She buffed them too, until they had a high shine; she might have worn nail polish of a color to match her lipstick (they sold those sets at the cosmetic counter at the back of the store), but the management did not allow that.

She had money of her own now, and the delicious expectation of each week's pay. (Dutifully she gave half to her mother, the rest was hers.) Sometimes she would stand for long minutes, half-smiling, half-dozing, smoothing the bills between her manicured fingers, pressing the coins against her palms until they left their imprint on her skin.

Every evening on the streetcar home, she stared through the dirty finger-smeared window, lulled by the steady rocking, and dreamed half-visions of the future. She had never done that before. She had met only one day at a time, fearful. Now she saw the future, a series of busy days. Beyond grimy windows the littered crowded streets were mysteriously inviting. She lived now in a state of great excitement, with a fluttering in her stomach, a feeling of endless energy, a sense that flowers were beautiful and rain was lovely, that colors were brighter than they had ever been before, that something wonderful was about to happen. She had no experience of it, but she thought this must mean that she was happy.

One day John Denham walked past Woolworth's big front window. They stared and blinked and then laughed at the sight of each other grown up. They had been children together; he'd lived two blocks away. In those half-remembered days before her father's death, they had played and adventured together. "When you get off work," he said, "I'll be waiting for you." He rode home with her on the streetcar, but he wouldn't come near her house. "Your mama wouldn't like me."

"Why not?"

"She won't like any boy hanging around you. I'll see you after work tomorrow."

He did, every evening. They talked the whole way home, nervously, rapidly summarizing the years. He told her that years ago his family had moved across town to share a house with his aunt. "Way out," he said. "Nothing but swamps behind us. We used to go crawfishing a lot." Once, he told her, he'd gone back to their old neighborhood and people said she'd gone off to the convent.

"I thought you were going to be a nun," he said.

"Not me." She held up her soft manicured hands, admiring them against the scratched varnish of the car seats. "Mama went to work but she couldn't make enough to keep me and the house both, and then Father Lauderman heard that the convent needed somebody, and that somebody turned out to be me."

"They teach you anything?"

"Sure. Cooking—would you believe they've got thirty-seven nuns there. And embroidery and crochet. And a lot of prayers."

"Okay," he said, "say me a prayer."

"I get plenty enough prayers in church on Sunday," she said. "Anyway, the next stop is mine."

He got off with her and they stood talking until a car came going the other way. He swung on, she walked home.

And so she saw him six days a week. She learned that he still lived at home with his parents and his orphaned cousins and his grandmother. That he'd finished Jesuit High School and right away was lucky enough to get a job with the post office, delivering mail. "I like it," he said. "I couldn't ever stand being inside at a desk all day long."

"I like my job too," she said.

"What do you do on Sundays?"

"Go to mass. Do my laundry and my ironing and be sure my clothes are ready for the week. And I help my mother with her garden, and in the evenings there's always the radio programs."

"You don't work much in the garden, not with hands like that."

"I didn't know you noticed my hands."

"Sure I notice. I notice everything about you."

She felt pleased and shy.

"But your Sundays don't sound like any fun to me."

"I like it just the way it is," she said. But in truth she didn't like it as much as she had.

"Where do you go to church? St. Rita's?"

"Mama and I go to the eleven o'clock every Sunday, rain or shine. She wouldn't miss it."

"What would you say if I told you I'd be there? That'd surprise you, wouldn't it? Well, I used to go to that church when I was a kid living just down the street from you, and I might just take myself back there again. Oh, I wouldn't talk to you, just spy on you. I know they get a big crowd for mass, so you see if you find me. And I bet you can't."

On Monday he said triumphantly, "You had a blue skirt and a white blouse and a tie like a man's, and you had to sit in the middle of a pew because you got there late, and you dropped your purse because you were so busy looking for me."

"I don't think that is a funny game," she said.

"I'm tired of it too." He popped a match against his thumbnail and lit a cigarette. "Let's not go to church next Sunday. Let's go out to the lake and walk along the seawall and have a look at all the big boats. I'll meet you at the streetcar stop at the end of Prentiss Street."

She did not meet him. She felt tired and out of sorts that Sunday, but she worked very hard in the garden, spraying the tomato plants with tobacco water to control aphids, staking and tying the beans.

"You are such a big help," her mother said. "You've got such a lot of energy."

The following day John Denham said, "You sure did miss a good time yesterday."

"I told you I was busy."

"Sure you were," he said. "I'll believe anything."

Day after day he waited for her. "Who's your boyfriend?" the other girls at Woolworth's asked. "He's not a boyfriend, he's just somebody used to live in my neighborhood."

The September rains began and he carried a big gray post office umbrella. The interior of the streetcars smelled of wet mud and musty sawdust, but the windows were washed clean by the pounding rain.

"You can't work in that precious garden now," he said.

"Not much any more," she said.

"So let's go out this Sunday."

"I am busy on Sundays," she said. "I have very important things to do."

"What's more important than me?"

She hesitated, not wanting to tell him, not really, but telling him anyway. "I crochet."

"All day? You're crazy."

"No." This time she didn't try to explain how pleasant Sundays were—with the street quiet and empty except for a few wandering dogs. Even kids' games sounded muted on Sundays, without so much screaming. She'd sit on the front porch with her mother, while Joseph read the newspaper and then, finished, slept soundly in his special rocking chair. Sometimes they were so silent and still that mourning doves perched on the railing and watched them. In chilly weather they sat in the parlor. Joseph dozed in the chair that he had brought in from the porch, the bright red patterned cushions almost hidden by his bulk. Her mother read aloud from the *State Times* or the *Diocesan Chronicle*, news of weddings and births and deaths. She herself sat surrounded by baskets of yarn, all colors, pale sea green her favorite. Her crochet hook flashed faster and faster, in and out, catching, dragging, snaring. The soft wool nets slipped away from her hands, completed.

"Okay," John said, "so what do you crochet that takes all day, every Sunday."

"They're called fascinators," she said. "You saw me wearing one the other day."

"That head scarf thing?"

"Not a scarf," she said. "They're pretty and they're warm. I always used to wear mine to church, I made them in two or three different colors to match the altar vestments."

"What?"

"It seemed respectful," she said. "Well, ladies began stopping me, wanting to know where I got them, because the department stores don't have anything nearly so nice. I made some for them, and I found I could do it very fast. So I put a notice in the *Chronicle*. Now I take orders, any color if you bring me the wool and any stitch if you show me what it is. I've got lots of orders for Christmas. People don't mind what they spend at Christmas."

"Money," he laughed, "is that all you ever think about? You got a job and you still want more."

"I've been poor," she said slowly, trying to explain, "and the convent took me in and the nuns taught me needlework, all kinds of needlework. It was like they were making me a present of it. And I can use it now."

"You are plain crazy," he said.

Still, every day after work he waited at the streetcar stop. It was December now, with cold winter rain. The early azaleas showed their buds and the sasanquas opened their flat pink and white flowers.

"Something likes this weather," she said to him, pointing to the gardens as they passed.

"Not me," he said. "Look," he said, "make one of those fascinators for me and I'll give it to my mother for Christmas. She'll be expecting something."

"Okay," she said.

"They look kind of pretty on you, so maybe they'll do something for her too."

She felt herself flushing, as pleased as if it had been a proper compliment.

After Christmas the rain stopped. In the parks camellias bloomed and all the big purple azaleas.

"Come to the park with me this Sunday," he said. "We'll look at those flowers you're so crazy about and then we'll go to the aquarium and watch them feed the seals."

"I work on Sunday," she said primly.

"You're not still making those stupid scarfs," he said. "Christmas is over."

"I'm making baby dresses."

"Don't tell me the nuns taught you that."

"They taught me to smock," she said. "People want real smocking on their baby clothes and I add little embroidered rosebuds too."

"And people buy that?"

"All I can make," she said.

"Okay," he said. "I'm going to walk by your house this Sunday and I am going to see."

"You're checking up on me," she said, and was flattered by the thought. "If you walk past I am going to pretend I don't know you."

"What makes you think I'm going to talk to you?" he said. "I just want to look."

He did. He walked by slowly, looking at the houses on both sides. She did not lift her head from her work, not even when he walked back again.

"I hope you are satisfied," she said.

"You are crazy, I knew it."

"No."

"You don't ever think of me, I bet. You won't even miss me when I'm gone."

She stared at him. "Where are you going?"

"Got your attention that time, didn't I? You heard about this little thing called the draft, and yours truly is 1A. They're going to haul me off any day now."

"I forgot."

"Well, old Uncle Sam ain't going to let me forget. Hey, look, next stop is yours. You better ring the bell."

They stood talking longer than usual that day, leaning against the rough trunk of one of the young oak trees at the corner.

"I bet you won't even miss me when I'm out there getting shot at."

"There ain't any war," she said, "not unless you know something I don't."

"They're drafting an army," he said. "You don't make an army if you don't plan to use it."

The last azaleas faded, purple wisteria ran wild along the fences, lost its flowers and put out its leaves; high up on the old buildings the Rose of Montana vine began to show its small pink flowers. Then one day he wasn't waiting at the streetcar stop, and she rode home alone. He wasn't there the next day, or the next. The weather turned stormy, fishing boats scurried back into port. It rained so heavily that the streets flooded and she waded home in waist-deep water. By morning the water was down; children were fishing for crawfish in the ditches, all of them playing hooky from school.

Finally he was back, thin and tired-looking. "I got my induction notice," he said, "four or five other guys too. We all took annual leave and got drunk. Then we took the train to Chicago just for the ride."

She wasn't too sure exactly where Chicago was, though she did remember learning about it in geography class. So he had just gone off like that, to a spot on the map. . . .

"We decided we didn't much like Chicago so we came back. Here's your streetcar, didn't you notice?"

Again he disappeared without a word.

"What happened to your boyfriend?" Norma, who sold cosmetics, asked.

"The army," she said. "And he's not my boyfriend."

Norma lifted her eyebrows. "Too bad."

Evenings Willie May rode home alone, feeling strange and a little hurt that he had not said good-bye. He shouldn't have just disappeared, she thought.

Joseph retired from the police force, complaining of pains in his chest. The doctor told him to stop drinking beer and lose weight; her mother fussed over him, fixing special meals which Joseph wouldn't eat. She hid his beer. He started spending afternoons at the Paradise Bar, two blocks away. He liked their draft, he said, a lot better than bottles.

Willie May herself had so many orders for children's dresses that her mother had to help with the cutting and some of the simple sewing and the ironing and the folding in tissue paper. And she still worked at Woolworth's. In the summer heat, the air in the store turned musty and sweaty and heavy. The tall fans barely pushed it along the aisles. The floorwalkers complained all day long about dust on the counters, and the clerks polished and rearranged them constantly. Aphids appeared like white frosting on all the potted coleus. Two stock boys took them to the back loading platform and dabbed at the bugs with rubbing alcohol.

In August Willie May got her first order for a christening dress, a peau de soie robe over a long lawn shift. She worked on it for a month, carefully dusting her hands with talcum powder so that her sweating fingers left no mark on the white material.

One Sunday as she and her mother sat on the porch and Joseph dozed in the hammock he had slung between two mulberry trees in the yard, John Denham sauntered up the walk and stood with one foot on the steps, grinning. His hair was so short that he seemed quite bald and he was in uniform. "I got leave," he said. "You want to take a ride out to the lake and get an ice cream?"

"I've got to finish the dress," she said.

Her mother took the material from her hands and carried it carefully inside.

He laughed. "Your ma says yes."

"I suppose so," she said. She was very confused and she did not like the feeling at all. "You surprised me," she said. "I don't like being surprised."

"Look, don't blame me," he said; "the army owns me now."

Her mother said from inside the screen door, "It will take her just a few minutes to freshen up. Would you like some iced tea, what did you say your name was?"

So they caught the streetcar to the lake and ate ice cream cones and walked along the seawall and looked at the muddy water and sat on benches under small pine trees and listened to a band play marches and waltzes and opera overtures. Children skated on the concrete walks and chalked the outlines of hopscotch games. The young women were there in their summer dresses, full skirted and starched crisp against the summer heat. The young men were in uniform.

"What's the matter with you," he said. "You're scowling."

She answered truthfully, "I felt afraid, all of a sudden."

He grinned and put his arm around her. "Baby, you got nothing to be afraid of when I'm with you."

"Oh," she said. And didn't tell him she knew he was wrong about that.

They settled finally on a shady bench near a fountain. They could hear the water trickling and bubbling in the wide basin.

"Look," he said. "You ever think about yourself? Like what you're going to do next? And why you want to do it?"

"No," she said.

"Well, you should. Now, you're a good-looking gal. A real pretty face and a nice figure even if you are too thin. But then, you can be pretty disagreeable and grumpy and you can set that mouth of yours tight like a nun."

She stared at him, anger beginning in a flush.

"But I still think we ought to get married."

She stopped, realized her mouth was open, and shut it with a click of teeth.

"It kind of makes sense. We get married, and you stay at your mother's house, and I come back when they give me leave. You keep working and if I get killed you get the insurance. I'm sure as hell worth more dead than alive."

Two children were running across the open field, their dresses bright multicolored spots on the green. Water dribbled from the bronze urn held high by a fat bronze boy on the edge of the fountain.

It isn't real, she thought.

"We go meet my family tonight. I already met yours. Tomorrow I see the priest and it'll all be arranged when I pick you up after work tomorrow. What do you say to that?"

"All right," she said. "Fine with me."

The banns were announced at three masses the next Sunday, and they were married that evening. It was just about the only free time the priest had, there were so many wedding on such short notice.

He came back twice on leave before war started and he was sent to England. Willie May left Woolworth's for a job at the shipyards. It was hard and dirty work—but she saved her money carefully and watched the total grow slowly month after month. In the second April of the war, her mother died in her sleep. Then Joseph remembered his children in Texas and grew lonesome for them and his grandchildren, and went to spend his last days with them. He did not write, so she never knew exactly how many last days he had.

There were few letters from John, but she did not worry. He was a headquarters clerk and they never got shot at, he told her. "I'm still handling the mail, only now I'm getting paid a lot less for doing it." He was a corporal, then a sergeant. "If you don't hear from me," he said, "you know I'm all right."

In a way she was glad he didn't write, nor expect her to write very often. She was just too tired. She worked the graveyard shift at the shipyards—the pay was better—and she never quite got used to sleeping in the daytime with children shouting just outside the window. Once she had her picture in the shipyards' paper: a group of four women, waving to a newly completed PT boat. She clipped that out and sent it to John. She did not sew or knit or crochet any more; her hands were too stiff and heavy. Occasionally, holding a pencil awkwardly, she would sketch a child's dress. She always felt better then, when she could dream about the clothes she would make one day for other people's children, lovely things she herself had never had.

When the war was over, she got a long letter from John, the only one ever. He'd been drinking, he said, and he'd been thinking. . . . There'd been some talk about them having to go into occupation forces, but the captain said that was just stupid, maybe the unit would go, but any guy with nearly five years' service could get out if he wanted to. . . . And he wanted to. "So one of these days you'll see me come walking up to the yard and maybe I'll have one of those big FOR SALE signs on my shoulder and we'll go for a paddle in the canal. Like we used to. You remember?"

She did. It was the best game of the long rainy summers of that faraway childhood.

First the oldest and the boldest and the strongest children gathered the large wood and metal signs one particular realtor installed at his buildings. C ME FOR SALE C. BELL the signs said in red and black letters. The children stole them from walls and lawns and hid them away until heavy rains filled all the drainage ditches and canals. Then each large sign became a raft for two children, their paddles the curved fronds of the tall palm trees.

Willie May smelled the freshness of rain-cleaned air and the nutty odor of her own sweat. She was aware also of the presence of another child. (Had that been John? She didn't know.) She saw her arms (long and thin and spotted with mosquito bites) and she saw the brush-burns on her knees (large dark scabs always bleeding). She was shivering with pride and excitement: the smell of drainage water, the smell of sweet decay, was the smell of freedom.

She was never afraid, though they all knew it was dangerous. Childhood sheathed her, protected her.

The children slid down the grass-spotted mud banks of open drainage ditches to launch their rafts on the slow-moving water. Buoyed by its wooden frame, the sheet of tin floated a fraction of an inch above the surface. Each stroke of the paddle sent a thin sheet of water across it.

Because the city was built on perfectly flat land, it was drained after every heavy rain by huge pumps concealed in brick buildings. (Keep out of the canals, all the mothers screamed, you'll drown, they'll pick you out of the screens at the pumping station with the drowned dogs and the drunks, and the runaways from the state hospital. . . . None of the children paid attention, though they once did see a body floating. The police were already there, grappling for it.)

The grassy ditches led into wider concrete-lined canals where rusting iron pipes high over their heads dripped small streams of water. Here the surface was slack and oily, showing only the faintest pull of the distant pumps.

Soon they passed under the High Street Bridge. A man named Duke, who worked in the gas station on that corner, had made himself guardian of that stretch of canal and watched it all day long. He'd rescued so many children from the water that newspapers often did stories about him. Willie May had seen pictures of him, beaming, dripping wet, holding a child in his arms. Sometimes he was too late; the children were drowned. He snagged their bodies with a long hooked pole and dragged them out. Then the newspaper picture showed him holding a small wrapped bundle.

Willie May remembered him clearly, shouting, leaning over the side of the bridge, one arm reaching down to catch them, a thick hairy arm with a hand so huge it filled the sky.

The children crouched down, swinging their palm frond paddles like bats against him. Sometimes they felt the air from his grasping arm against the backs of their necks. (If he caught you, he took your raft and sent you home.) "You'll kill yourself, you damn fool kids," he shouted. They shouted back at him in their high reedy voices, "No, no, no."

Farther down the canal there was a dark-haired woman who sat in her backyard under a medlar tree. She waved to them, silently.

Even farther along there was an old man, a very old man, who always wore a grayish bathrobe and held a glass of red liquid in his hand. He called to them, using the same words every time: "You pass on my canal, and you never stop to talk to me. Come talk to me and I will give you some cream soda." And he held up the red-filled glass and rattled the ice against its sides.

Though he was much too old and frail to chase them, they were afraid, and never looked directly at him as they passed. He might have the evil eye.

Now, listening carefully, they heard the sucking, gurgling sound of fast-moving water. They were nearing the point where their canal emptied into a still larger one, where the water was very swift and the pumps less than a mile away through a great brick-lined underground culvert.

Already ripples surged across the tin surface of their raft. They dug in their paddles, turned the raft into the side. They landed with a thump and a splash. Quickly, they scrambled up the slope and stood on the concrete parapet to watch.

The empty raft, freed of their weight, floated off. It slipped into the main canal, its prow bobbing, nodding to itself, as trickles of water splashed across its tin deck. The raft shifted from side to side, anxiously, nervously, then began spinning in circles, traveling faster and faster. Until it vanished into the darkness of the brick tunnel.

Willie May and the other child watched it disappear, their adventure half over, only the trip home left. Stretching and whistling, arms out, they pranced like acrobats along the narrow concrete edge. Tiring of that, they wandered through strange yards, teasing dogs, stealing medlars or pomegranates or figs, according to the season. At Calhoun Street, at the traffic light, they hitched rides on the backs of trucks, hunched down carefully out of the drivers' sight. If they were very lucky, they might catch an iceman's truck and find a handful of ice flakes under the dark canvas.

Among those children had been John Denham, her husband. He remembered, even if she didn't. But then she always had trouble remembering John. When he walked into her living room that November day in 1945, still in uniform, duffel bag on his shoulder, she blinked with surprise. He'd never seemed quite real to her.

He went back to work in the post office. She was pregnant three months later with a boy, their only child, named Michael.

While she waited for his birth, while her body grew thick and full and her work-stiffened hands became soft and pliable again, she began setting up her own business: children's dresses. She got out the designs that she had drawn so awkwardly during the war years, and she selected the best, carefully, lovingly. Her designs were always ornate, the colors always unusual—her clothes would be easy to recognize. A year later she sold the first of her special christening dresses, one with a cape of seed pearls to be used later in a wedding veil. For that, because she did it herself alone, there was a waiting period of five months.

"Those women are crazy enough to order that far in advance?" John said. "My God, Willie May, they've got to call you as soon as they find out they're pregnant."

"Yes," she said smugly, "they do."

"But our kid didn't have a fancy dress when he got baptized."

"I didn't have the time," she said with a smile.

She hired three women, then five, and that was all.

John said, "If you advertised, you could sell a hell of a lot more. You could have a real factory, not just five people, you could be growing."

She shook her head. "I don't want to advertise, I want the mothers and the grandmothers to hear about me. I want them to see my dresses and then want to buy them. Sure, I could hire more people right now, but I want the customers to wait. They will. The Mary Lynne Shop gave me an order yesterday, even when I told them it would be four months before delivery."

"Crazy," John said.

"No," she said, "they know my clothes are hard to get and expensive."

"And they like that?"

"Yes," she said, "that's exactly what they want."

Their son, Michael, was healthy and strong, polite in his catechism class and good in school. The three of them lived quietly, well-organized and orderly. Every Sunday after ten o'clock mass they went to John's family for midday dinner. Sunday afternoons they went for drives in their new Plymouth, stopping in the park to watch the child play. They went to a downtown movie on Saturday night and Bingo on Thursday. John went out with the boys on Friday night. Sometimes he did not come back to the house at all, but went directly to work on Saturday morning. He kept his post office uniform neatly folded in the trunk of his car.

Eventually those Friday evenings became whole weekends. Willie May scarcely noticed. She still took their son downtown on Saturday evenings to the big movie house with its curving stairs and crystal chandelier and velvet curtains. And she went to John's family for Sunday dinner, saying only, "John won't be here." His parents never asked about him.

She decided on a name for her company. Until then her dress labels carried only three gold fleurs-de-lis (she'd seen them on the banner of St. Louis King of France). Now she added *Beatrix Designs*, named for the author of Michael's favorite book, *Peter Rabbit*.

Somewhere in those years, once, John asked, "You want to take a vacation? I got all this annual leave coming to me. I got to use it or lose it."

"I don't know of any place I want to go," she said slowly.

"A couple of the boys are talking about driving over to Morrisport for some fishing. We can rent a camp there. And I might just go."

"Fine," she said.

Quicker than she thought possible, Michael was finishing high school, and John took fishing vacations several times a year. It took her a couple of days to notice that he had not returned from one of them. Only then did she discover that his clothes were gone.

Feeling oddly embarrassed, as if she were peeping into an uncurtained window, she asked his family about him. He had retired, they said; he had twenty years' service.

She supposed he still lived in town, but it did not occur to her to look for him. The boy she had played with, sailing the drainage ditches after a heavy rain, the young man who had appeared at the counter in Woolworth's, the soldier who had walked into her house—they were all different, detached, set apart by time. They were none of them connected to the balding, middle-aged husband and father.

These things, they were all of them beyond her reach. Forces changing her life, and beyond her control. Impersonal, like wind and rain. Unquestioned.

Why should she be thinking of John now? . . . She had not taken a Seconal last night and so she'd been up very early, long before day showed the other side of the drawn hospital blinds.

"Good morning, Mrs. Denham. Your son's already called to tell us that he's on his way."

"I will be glad to leave."

She let her eyes wander lazily around the room, across the pictures—soft landscapes and seascapes—the two large chairs, the flowers.

A better room to die in, she thought, than ever I was born in. But I don't die here today. Today I go home.

Whispering rubber voices of wheelchairs across polished corridor floors. Into cars. Into other corridors and other cars. Endless whispering.

Long before she boarded the plane, she was so tired she could scarcely hold her head upright.

It will be too much for me, she thought, I should not have tried. It will be too much for me. I shall die on the way. But no, I didn't drown on the raft all those years ago. I balanced and paddled and reached the end and got home safely.

Propped against the vibrating plane wall she dozed, woke to pain. Michael was there. "Here, Mother." White pills and a fuzziness that did not change the pain, only pushed it farther away. As if it were happening to somebody else. In another place, another time.

Michael said, "Mother, this is Dallas. We'll be here for a little while. Would you like a change of scene? Would you like to see the new airport?"

Look at something I will never see again? No. I have seen enough. I carry enough images inside my head to need no more.

My world grows smaller, the edges peel back, an orange shedding its skin.

But who would think an hour could be so long... Time doesn't rush toward its end. It groans and creaks and creeps along. Like the beat and the wheeze of the heart, its clock. Each tick like a slow hammer stroke, a gong sounding to mark something or other. Whatever.

She opened her eyes and saw people in the plane as skeletons, she saw right through their flesh, saw their bones, saw their blood running through its appointed channels.

She thought: Were I ever so small, a microbe, a molecule, I would ride my raft along those red courses, I would follow those warm canals, exploring.

She floated on the warm canals, she saw the flaws in the bone, inspected them carefully: the chips and the old breaks and the dusty grit of arthritis. She noted them all, and also the swirls and the eddies and the cumbersome debris all along the warm red courses.

Long before the plane left Dallas, she herself left the ground, flying. The air was soft, silvery birds flew so close to her that their feathers tickled her cheeks. She brushed them away.

Michael said, "Mother?"

But he was not with her, he was far away, held in the plane, and his voice was faint.

She was flying, alone, complete. She saw rushing toward her, rushing past her, everything. Leaves uncurled, people rose from their beds. Cats crouched, claws tearing fur across backs. Copulation: a jumble of arms and legs. She saw hospitals and bodies lying open and bloody until they were sewed back together missing some part or other. She saw rain falling and snow falling and flowers opening their buds like ticking clocks. She saw people brushing their teeth and people weeping in corners. She saw police dozing in squad cars. She saw bitches strain in birth and puppies born like chains of pearls. She saw suns rise and stars dance in their paths across the seasons. She saw ants and oceans and curving endless space. She saw her house, the one she had lived in all her life. She saw a leaf fallen in the gutter. And swamp water bubbling with its own gases, shivering with the swarms of life beneath.

Secure in her power and boastful of her strength, she raced the plane home. And won.

She was waiting at the airport when Michael pushed her wheelchair through the gates. She sniffed at the thin figure sagging sideways, dribble of saliva draining from the mouth, eyes half open but unseeing.

Filled with distaste, she joined them for one more, the last, passage in this trip. Another trailing hiss of rubber wheels across shiny machine-polished floors, another car, another ride.

She grew impatient with their progress and tried to lift

herself from the car to float on the layers and levels of the wind. This time she could not. Her power drained, she was trapped inside the tin shell, inside her shattered body.

Michael was there and Michael would let her out. Michael would open the door as soon as they reached home. Until then the endless pale concrete highways, looping rises and the turnoffs, dark night and day all one and the same. Sun and shade. Highways like ribbons, streams of concrete.

They stopped finally and Michael opened the doors and lifted her out.

She was too tired now to rise and soar and find the wind. She would need help. In the sky there seemed to be something . . . a kite. She could ride a kite.

"Is that a kite, Michael? Over there in the sky?"

"No, Mother," he said, "there isn't anything there."

There were other people, but she did not bother noticing them. She stayed hidden behind her eyelids, thinking about all the roads she had traveled that day, the twists and turns that had brought her home. And this was her house, she knew it by its smell. She was home. She smiled to herself, ignoring the distant voices. Was that Michael calling? Well, she would not answer.

She discovered that she was floating, lightly, delicately, on water flickering and iridescent with oil film. Was somebody with her? John? But John was dead years ago. She was alone. Her body was small and light and when she dabbled her fingers in the water, her hand was a sunburned child's hand. The day was sunny and there was a very slight breeze. In the sky there were fluffy white clouds that people called bishops, they were so fat and smug and self-important looking. The water flowed swiftly, carrying her past familiar trees: fig and medlar branches drooping with out-of-season fruit. The bridge now, the High Street Bridge. There was no one on it today, no hand stretched down to bring children home safe from danger. The water made little cooing, coaxing sounds. . . . Past the spot where the old man sat, the old man who offered them cream soda to stop and talk to him. No one tempted her today. The raft was moving very fast now, streams of water like banners on each side.

Here was the end of the familiar journey, here was where they always paddled to the side and scrambled away home. But now she had no paddle. And the current was swifter than she ever remembered. No stopping. The raft moved lightly, steadily, floating like a leaf, turning gently, seeming to know its way.

She had never been here, where the water was wide and the sun sparkled on tiny surface waves. She had never dared come this far before and she was astonished at how easy it was, how smooth and how silent.

The raft began to spin in circles, the sun and the clouds flickered across the sky. On both sides was the cream color of hospital walls, and there was nothing to see on them, only rising emptiness.

Then, as she knew she must, she saw the tunnel ahead. Just as she had seen it from the banks of childhood. She looked at it wonderingly, unsrprised. It waited. The raft sailed directly into it, into the dark.

A NOTE ON THE TYPE

The text of this book was set in a digitized version of Fournier, a typeface originated by Pierre Simon Fournier fils (1712–1768). Coming from a family of typefounders, Fournier was an extraordinarily prolific designer both of typefaces and of typographic ornaments. He was also the author of the celebrated Manuel typographique (1764–1766). In addition, he was the first to attempt to work out the point system standardizing type measurement that is still in use internationally.

The cut of the typeface named for this remarkable man captures many of the aspects of his personality and period. Though it is elegant, it is also very legible.

Composed by Crane Typesetting Service, Inc., Barnstable, Massachusetts.
Printed and bound by Maple-Vail Book Group, Binghamton, New York.
Designed by Betty Anderson.